THEIR SHIFTER PRINCESS

MAY DAWSON

PROLOGUE

A*lmost eighteen years ago...*

"It's a girl!"

Even from her bedroom, Angelica heard the roar of joy that went up from the pack, and it made her smile. The newborn had already fallen asleep again, her round cheek squished against her mother's breast. Rain pounded the house, beating against the roof so hard that even she had barely been able to hear her groans in labor, but even with the storm raging outside, she felt peace.

David returned to the bedroom and closed the door behind him. A smile still played across his lips. The pack had celebrated the birth of each son in the new generation, from Callum on down to Nicholas just a few months earlier. But born shifter girls were rare, for some reason, and it was a special source of pride to have brought the first girl into Blissford Manor.

"How is she?" He carefully slid under the blankets beside his wife and newborn child, although he leaned on his elbow, because he wanted to look at their faces. Angelica's wildly curly hair was mussed from the birth, and she'd drawn it into a haphazard knot on top of her head. Her face in profile was the sweetest thing he'd ever seen... except perhaps for the red-cheeked face of his daughter, with her long lashes and bald head. He'd never found newborns to be particularly cute before, but her first desperate cries entering this world had broken his heart and filled it with light all at once.

"She's fine." Angelica caressed the baby's face with her fingertips as if she were caught up in wonder. Her touch was so light that the baby slept on peacefully.

There was a soft tap on the door. Angelica added, "But I could use a cheeseburger. That was a lot of work, you know."

"Of course." David dropped a kiss in her hair and went to the door.

When he swung it open, Callum stood there. He leaned in the doorway, his freckled face—under a mop of dark hair— curious to catch a glimpse of the pack's new little princess. David blocked his view, filling the doorway as he smiled teasingly. "Yes, Callum?"

"Do you need anything?" Callum asked.

"Well—"

There was a *bang* from somewhere downstairs that shook the house. The rain had pounded the house all night, terrible crashes of thunder and lightning rocking the outside while Angelica panted with the midwives and he paced. Lightning must have stuck the house. Then the tingle of dark magic burned across his skin.

This was no storm. This was an attack.

The little kids, Josh and Kai and the baby Nick, would be sleeping in the nursery room at the other end of the house while the adults celebrated downstairs. "Protect the cubs until their parents can take over."

Without hesitation, Callum turned and sprinted down the hall.

David turned toward the bed, but Angelica was already struggling from the soft mattress, holding her baby tight to her chest.

The sounds of battle raged downstairs, the crackle of magic and the growls and fury of wolves.

"They're coming for her," he said.

Angelica laid the baby in the white crib by the windows. The baby woke up and began to cry at the sudden cold and being separated from her mother.

"Shh, sweetheart," Angelica said. "Mama loves you."

She didn't dare make any promises. In the distance, she could hear a yelp as a wolf went down. She couldn't be sure from the cry who it was. Her brother? Their alpha?

David gave her a quick, anguished glance over his shoulder. He didn't have time to say goodbye to his daughter. He was already snarling as he bounded toward the door, ready to tear apart any witch who tried to steal his daughter.

Angelica longed to sweep her lips over her daughter's downy hair one last time, but her fingers tightened on the edge of the crib as she began to shift. The change made her shoulders curl forward, her elbows braced on the railing as her knee joints snapped, reversing themselves. The pain was excruciating—every time—like nails being driven through her body, but then it was gone, lost in the adrenaline of the change. She turned and threw herself down to the floor, and when her hands hit the hardwood floor, they were paws.

The baby was screaming. The sound pierced her ears painfully. She leapt up onto her hind legs, catching the rail with her paws. Angelica's deep blue eyes met her newborn daughter's gaze. Her daughter stared up at her in wonder, her lips parted, no longer crying.

Newborns couldn't see well, but she had to believe her daughter saw her, once. That her daughter saw her future.

The baby was quiet until the door flew open. One witch, then two more, stepped into the room. Angelica leapt at them, and a crack of magic boomed in the narrow space, setting the baby to frantic tears again. Angelica ripped out the throat of one witch, already whirling on the next... but it was always a lost cause.

The coven leader made it a point to step over the mother wolf's body on his way to the crib. He wrapped his hands around her rib cage and scooped up the mewling baby. She was crying frantically now, a desperate bleating sound, her head lolling forward helplessly.

"You don't look like much," he said, "but you are going to be very useful to me."

He laid her on his chest, patting her back absent-mindedly, and turned to carry her past the carnage of what had been the Blissford pack. "Let's get you home, daughter."

1

P*iper*

I WAS WALKING Maddie to school when I spotted trouble ahead. Trouble in the form of Eli Kingston and his two best friends, or should I say *lackeys*. The three of them were walking *toward* us, away from the high school, so they'd probably come looking for me.

"Hey kiddo," I said, resting my hand on Maddie's shoulder. We were only a block away from the elementary school.

She looked up at me. Her blue eyes were wide and dark-lashed, her face innocent under her pigtails. I wanted to make sure she stayed that way, no matter what kind of trouble I was in.

Sometimes, that meant I lied. I did whatever it took to protect her.

"I'll race you to school," I told her. "All the way to do the door. You up for it?"

She crinkled her nose at me. "You're so slow."

"And you're so short, but I don't bring it up all the time." I rested my hand on top of her head affectionately. "If I fall behind, you go ahead into school. I don't want to make you late."

Her heart-shaped face clouded, and a spike of guilt stabbed into my chest. Maddie took fourth grade very seriously. She'd never be late on purpose. Reading was an escape for her, and school was a haven. We shared a love of books.

"We're going to be late?" she asked in alarm.

"Not you, since you're so fast," I said, my voice teasing. "Ready, set..."

She positioned her arms, one forward and one back, like a little sprinter. She *also* had my competitive streak.

"Go!" I said, exploding forward myself. Together, the two of us sprinted across the sidewalk. I always felt a rise of joy at my sneakers hitting the pavement and pushing away, and racing my little sister made me feel like a kid.

Except I was running right toward danger.

Maddie went past them as I slowed, falling back just enough to keep an eye on her. I stepped onto the grass, trying to avoid Eli, and he turned, his eyes following me. A mean grin came to his lips.

I made it two steps past him, before powerful arms closed around me from behind. I stumbled, trying to get loose, but he moved with me. His hot breath blew against my ear.

"Don't scream," he said. "That little girl looks back and I'm going to snatch her up too."

"Let go of me," I said fiercely.

He finally did, pushing me away from him. I took a quick step forward, ready to run, but the three of them surrounded me. They boxed me in, pressing closer and closer. Eli's big-jawed, grinning face hovered too near mine.

I looked toward the elementary school. Maddie's hot pink backpack bounced up and down on her back as she turned in the gate. There were teachers around the school, directing students off busses. She was safe.

No one looked my way, though.

"Let's walk together," Eli said companionably, throwing an arm over my shoulders. He hugged me close to his side, and I breathed in the overwhelming scent of his cologne, which was so strong it tickled the back of my throat. I coughed under my breath.

He thought I was easy prey. Maybe that was why he'd become so obsessed with me. But he didn't know me as well as he thought.

"You stood me up this weekend," he said.

"My dad doesn't let me date. I told you that."

"You're almost eighteen," he said it like I was stupid.

"Oh, I know."

He squeezed my shoulders, tight enough to hurt, trying to punish me for my tone. From my peripheral vision, I could see Dan covering him, just a step behind and on my right.

There was half a mile between us and the high school. There wasn't much protection at school, either; Eli's father was kind of a big deal. He owned one of the two plants in town.

"Did you even ask your daddy?" he drawled. The word sounded revolting coming from him. It would have sounded revolting anyway, because my father had never been warm and caring. Even when I was little, he was never a *daddy,* and he sure wasn't one now. "I'll bet he would let you go out with me."

My father owned the *other* plant. He and Eli's father were drinking buddies.

"He's not going to say yes," I told him firmly. "We've got rules."

Unlike in Eli's family.

"You should have snuck out," he chided. "We would have had fun."

If I were going to risk a beating, it wouldn't be to hang out with Eli Kingston, that was for damn sure.

"You hurt my feelings." He said it lightly, like he was playing with me, but I was sure it was true. He needed to shave, but the faint scraggle across his jaw was wispy. Despite how toned and muscular he was, there was a bit of pudge in his cheeks still. I'd hurt the man-baby's feelings.

"Why me?" I asked. "You could have any girl in school, Eli."

Might as well appeal to the boy's vanity.

It might be true, though. I didn't understand why he was drawn to me, when I wanted nothing more than to read my books, keep to myself, and count down the days until I turned eighteen. But I couldn't seem to stay out of trouble.

"There's nothing quite like the sweet, innocent girl who's been protected by her daddy," he said. As his arm dropped off my shoulders, my posture straightened, my shoulders squaring. I sighed in relief at being released.

But his hand promptly found it way right to my ass. He rested his palm confidently on my jeans pocket, as if I belonged to him. His touch burned. Adrenaline spiked in my chest, restlessness flooded my legs. I couldn't *not* react.

"Then you should find one of those," I told him.

I stomped on his foot as hard as I could, shoving him away, already whirling to run. He fell backward. He was going to hit the sidewalk hard, but I wasn't going to hang around and watch.

Dan ran toward me as their other buddy, Red, dove to help Eli up.

Dan's eyes widened. Instead of running away, I stepped in toward him. His momentum carried him into me as I ducked suddenly. His thighs crashed into my arms as I threw them up to protect my head, and he flipped over me. The toe of his boot caught my ribs, hard enough that I heard a crack and I slammed down to my knees on the pavement. But despite the ache in my chest, and my kneecap burning, I pushed myself up and staggered forward.

I was already running before the three of them scrambled to their feet.

I'm only slow when I run with Maddie. My lungs ached from the cold air I sucked in as I sprinted for the safety of school. Their feet thundered behind me for a few hundred feet.

"Wait, wait," Eli barked. Suddenly, the noise behind me fell away.

The street ahead of me blurred, but I didn't see anything to make them stop. There were no cops or teachers or adults who gave a damn. I wasn't sure if there even were any adults in this town who would choose me and risk the wrath of the Kingstons. He must have some kind of new, awful plan.

But for now, I ran hard for school.

When I walked in the front door, my chest was still heaving. People gave me funny glances, then looked away.

In this town, I was the poor little rich girl. People were nice to me because of who my father is, but because of it, they weren't my friends, either.

In Homeroom, Mr. Turner looked up at me. His gaze lingered on my face, his expression troubled, and for a second, I thought he was going to ask me if I was okay. I was prepared to lie, but he looked down at his attendance log instead.

Misty Opal sat in the second row, her chair right ahead of mine. We used to be friends. Her eyes widened when they met mine. She looked like she was worried about me, like when we were kids and she realized I had one too many broken arms. My lips parted—although I didn't know what I was going to say—but Chelsey said something to her, and she leaned forward eagerly.

I let my backpack slide off my shoulder and groaned as I realize it had come unzipped sometime during my sprint. I sat down in a hurry with it in my lap, rummaging through the contents. My wallet was missing. So was my expensive fancy calculator. God damn it. It had been a long day already and it wasn't even nine o'clock. I bit hard on my lip, trying to calm myself down.

"They're so cute," Misty said to Chelsey, the words faintly registering for me.

"All three of them?"

"All three of them! It's like a variety pack of hotness."

I zipped my backpack up—for all the good it would do me now—and dropped it onto the floor between my feet. Then I leaned my head forward on my crossed arms on the desk, as if I could go to sleep. The world was red behind my eyelids as I breathed slowly, deeply, in and out.

Someone behind me leaned forward, and I caught an unfamiliar scent. The stale aroma of school was cleaning solution, dry erase markers, and a faint whiff of body odor, but this made my nostrils flare and I breathed deeper. It was old leather, automotive grease, clean, strong white soap and a hint of menthol aftershave. The smell was all *male*.

"You all right?" A low, warm voice asked, almost right in my ear.

I straightened, rubbing my hand across my face, and tried to look nonchalant as I twisted toward whoever was speaking to me.

It was a boy with mussed blond hair and a big square jaw. Bright blue eyes met mine evenly. They were the color of the ocean, vivid against his tanned skin.

He started to smile, and I realized I was staring. I never answered him.

"Yeah," I said. "Yeah, I'm fine."

"You just need a nap?" That playful smile tugged his lips a little higher.

"Give it two hours." He had to be new; I knew everyone in this school. It was an awfully small town. Well, really, it was an *awful* small town. "You'll need a nap too."

His lips widened, and then he really did smile. He had a nice grin above that determined jaw.

"You're new here," I said.

"I am," he said.

I'd just told him what he already knew. *Smooth, Piper.*

"I'm Josh." He stuck his hand out. Apparently, he was willing to be nice despite my having the social skills of a drunken hamster. "Nice to meet you."

"Piper." When I shook his hand, it was warm and dry. He had nice hands. I bit down on my lower lip, trying to focus on his face and making conversation instead of getting lost in thought about the guy's fingers. "Where are you from?"

"I just moved here from Portland, Oregon." He crossed his arms over his chest when he leaned back in his chair.

"That sounds like a cool town." *That sounds like a meaningless observation, Piper.* I didn't know anything about Portland. But I was committed now to the idea that Portland was Nirvana compared to Blissford. "You're about to have a rocky adjustment."

"It doesn't seem so bad so far." His eyes studied me carefully. "You're not happy here?"

I shrugged, trying to sound light-hearted, but I had the funniest feeling that Misty and Chelsey were listening as I embarrassed myself. "How many teenagers are happy in their hometown?"

"I was," he said.

"Then you didn't want to move?"

"I always believe in making the best of any situation." His straight, white teeth practically twinkled when he smiled. "I think I'll do okay here."

I bet he will.

Mr. Turner started talking, and I reluctantly turned my attention to the front of the class. Why had I turned so awkward the minute Josh's deep blue eyes met mine, then crinkled at the corners? I folded my hands on my desk and tried to contain my cringing. *You're new here. Portland is a cool town.*

I'm a complete imbecile.

I could have sworn I felt Josh's presence behind me when he shifted in his seat, when he leaned back and tapped his pencil against the desktop. Every little movement he made seemed to tug on my attention.

I was interested in following my plan, not in boys.

So why the hell was he so distracting?

2

The last thing I wanted to do at lunch was sit alone in the crowded, warm lunch room that smelled like hot dogs, with nothing to eat since I didn't have my wallet. Instead, I slipped outside. There was an open, hilly yard between the back of the school and the playing fields, with a handful of splintery picnic tables that were already occupied by groups of kids laughing with their friends. Some of them glanced at me as I headed toward a knot of trees, only their barren upper branches visible over the crest of the grassy hill. Sheltered from the sun and the wind, it was where I liked to hide to read my book sometimes. Luckily, one survivor of my earlier backpack mishap was the paperback tucked between textbooks.

I reached the top of the hill, and the three guys who sat under the trees came into view. When they looked up at me, their faces were curious and unwelcoming. My gaze bounced between them.

Josh was there, all wind-blown blond and ruddy cheeks. A tall, leanly-fit guy with dark hair leaned against one of the trees; his motorcycle boots were kicked out in front of him, his hands in his pockets. He met my gaze with intense brown eyes, and I looked quickly toward the next guy. He sat cross-legged in the grass, his dark brown curls ruffled by the breeze; his cheekbones were so sharp, his eyes so bright a green, that it was hard to tear my eyes away from him. I started to raise my hand to wave apologetically at interrupting them, because they didn't look friendly at all.

"Come sit down with us, Piper," Josh called. He gestured me over as the other two turned their cold stares on him.

I started to walk forward. It was only once I was committed that Josh said something to them, quietly, that I couldn't hear. The guy with the dark hair shook his head. I didn't want to go where I wasn't welcome, but Josh jumped up from the grass and strode toward me.

He smiled at me, that big square-jawed grin that made it hard to resist smiling back automatically. "You want to join us for lunch? We've got a pizza."

"It's your first day of school and you ordered delivery?" I asked lightly, trying to camouflage just how much I'd love a slice of pizza. My stomach growled, just faintly, and Josh cocked his head to one side.

"Yep," he said. "Got to start as you mean to go on."

"And you mean to go on with...Italian food?"

"I mean to do what I want in this school." He winked at me, resting a hand on my shoulder and steering me toward the other two guys and a white pizza box on the grass between them. "I don't plan to be miserable here. Even though it isn't Portland."

If there was one thing I'd learned growing up, it was that part of being young was being miserable.

"Sit," he told me. To his friends, he said, "You guys, be normal. Be social for once."

Reluctantly, the boy with the dark hair held out his hand. He had gorgeous deep brown, almond-shaped eyes, and his fitted black t-shirt clung to his muscular arms. "I'm Kai."

"Piper," I said, shaking his hand. He had a nice handshake, his hand firm and warm.

The boy with the curls nodded. "I'm Nick."

"You're all new here?" I asked. "Did you all move here together or did you just happen to meet up and form like, a new kid coalition?"

Kai stared at me so hard that I regretted ever using the words *new kid coalition.* At least when I had been awkward with Josh, he had pretended not to notice. "Do you always ask so many questions?"

Josh pushed gently on my shoulders, encouraging me to take a seat with them, and I sank cross-legged to the grass. He sat next to me, almost protectively close, then handed me a slice of pizza. Suddenly the air smelled of fresh-cooked bread and spicy red sauce, and I inhaled deeply. I'd skipped breakfast, like I often did—I couldn't eat in the morning until I'd had my coffee, and I was usually busy taking care of my sister—and the pizza was delicious.

"I only know one guy who does whatever he wants in this school," I said once I'd swallowed, glancing up the hill toward the school. I couldn't see Eli. He'd be holding court in the lunch room with the popular kids.

I was always welcome to sit with them, but the catty relationships between the girls and the outright harassment from Eli and his buddies was a whole lot worse than sitting alone.

"Well, I guess I'll have to dethrone him then," Josh said, smiling easily. I wasn't sure if he was joking or not.

"Senior year, right?" I asked him, and he nodded. "Hell of a time to shake things up."

"It's always a good time to shake things up," he said.

I stole a glance at Kai and Nick. Nick was stuffing pizza into his mouth with one hand—he managed to look cute even with his cheek as full as a chipmunk—and had picked up a book, which he held open, pinned against his knee.

Kai stared back at me, his eyes full of challenge. What a weirdo. I guessed we weren't going to be regular lunch buddies. When he went on staring at me, I widened my eyes at him, pulling a face. He glanced away, his mouth tightening.

"Do you know Misty?" Josh asked cheerfully.

"I know everyone. It's not that big a school." Did Josh have a crush on Misty, already? It wouldn't surprise me. Misty was bubbly and sweet and magnetic. Everyone liked her. Even now, when our friendship had been broken, there were times she'd meet my eyes and grin, as if she knew I'd get whatever she was thinking. I'd smile back before I remembered. She always looked away, like that moment of connection was an accident. Like she was embarrassed.

Josh shot a meaningful look at Kai and Nick.

"Do you like her?" My tone matched his for cheerfulness, but for some silly reason, there was an ache in my chest at the thought.

"I wouldn't mind getting to know her better," Josh said. "It's a little early to *like* anyone, since I've been at this school for fifteen minutes."

"What's her type?" Kai asked.

Wow, it was a good day for Misty. Either Kai was trying to help his friend out or he liked her too, and they were both stupid-gorgeous. It was weird how three guys this good-looking and fit and mysterious had all started school at the same time. But for now, I'd answer their questions. I'd figure these three out eventually.

"She likes athletic guys." She had a thing for guys dressed out for soccer or basketball. I knew that from the days we used to play soccer together.

Kai groaned, beneath his breath, and my gaze swiveled to him just before Nick said, "Looks like we're watching Varsity Blues tonight."

"No," Kai said.

"Oh yes," Nick said.

I didn't know what the hell was going on, but an intriguing, vibrant energy lingered between them. I checked my watch, reluctant to leave their magnetic pull and go back toward school. I should give them space though, since that seemed as though that was what Nick and Kai wanted.

"Did you move here from Portland?" I asked Nick, and he glanced at Josh before he said, "Yes."

These guys were pretty, but they were not exceptional conversationalists. At least, not with anyone beside each other.

"We're like brothers," Josh explained to me. "More or less. Nick is my brother, and Kai is my cousin. Our parents were driving together when they were killed by a drunk driver. So we all live with our uncle, Callum."

The way he rattled off those awful facts felt rehearsed, but I would be a terrible person if their tragic story was true and I doubted them. Plus, why would they lie about something like that? I chewed my lower lip. "Where do you live?"

"Why?" Kai asked.

Josh shot him a glare. "As long as we're asking *why*. Why are you like this?"

Kai shrugged. "I don't want to be here, you know that. I just want to keep my head down and..." he shot Josh a look I couldn't quite decipher, "graduate."

These guys were gorgeous and magnetic.

And really, really weird.

3

That evening, as I worked on my Pre-Calc homework, the doorbell chimed downstairs. I bit on the end of my pencil, hard enough that my teeth sank deep into the yellow paint, before I caught myself. Maybe it was nothing. Maybe it was Girl Scouts selling cookies.

"Piper!" my father bellowed. His voice carried all the way upstairs and through the door of my room like we weren't in a four-thousand-square-foot McMansion.

"Coming!" I called back immediately, jumping from my chair. But once I was standing, I wracked my brain, trying to think of a way out.

Even if he was going to hurt me tonight, it could serve a purpose. That was the thing that made it easier to survive lately. My father only seemed to grow more hateful the closer we came to my birthday.

I ran to my bookcase, fumbling for the teddy bear with wide black eyes that hid among the other stuffed animals on the shelf. I'd found the NannyCam at the thrift store—despite all my father's wealth, he hated to give me any money of my own—and as soon as I'd picked it up and realized what I held, the seeds of a plan started to blossom.

Of course, if he found out what I was doing, I'd be in worse trouble than ever before. I was playing a dangerous game, but it was the only way I could take care of Maddie.

I stepped into the hallway. Maddie's door remained closed. She was at a sleepover at her best friend's house, thank God. My father didn't hit her often—not like he hit me. He was easier on the baby of the family. She got to leave the house more than I did, too, even though I was ten years' older.

"Piper!" my father shouted again.

"I'm coming!" I called, running down the stairs.

I was only halfway down when I saw my father's back, and behind him, standing in the entryway, Eli and his father. Mr. Kingston had his hand on his son's shoulder, as if his little boy—who was six-foot-two—was some kind of victim.

My father turned to me, his eyes full of fury. "Did you *attack* Eli?"

The truth was often not my friend in this house, but my lips still parted. The desire to defend myself raged, and my chest tightened. But I had to be smart. *Survivor, you're a survivor,* my inner cheerleader reminded me. I could fight through anything. For Maddie. For our future.

And this was how I fought: with my wits and my courage and my willingness to fake it.

"Not exactly," I said. The one thing that might win my father to my side was how much he hated the thought of anyone getting too close to me. "Eli asked me out. He wouldn't take *no* for answer."

My father's lips tightened.

"I'm sure Eli was a gentleman," Mr. Kingston said. "Girls these days. Always looking for something to overreact to."

My father gazed at him blandly. The two of them were good friends, or at least, they spent a lot of time together. I wasn't sure either of them really had friends.

"She pushed me," Eli said calmly, crossing his arms. "I didn't mean any disrespect to her or to you, sir. I'm sorry if she misunderstood me."

"I told him I'm not allowed to date," I said doggedly. "And he put his arm around me."

"I brought this back." He held out my Kate Spade wallet and my scientific calculator. "She dropped them on our way to school."

My father's eyes widened as he took in the two expensive things that Eli held out. Then his gaze flickered to me. I stepped forward and awkwardly took the two things out of Eli's outstretched hand, trying not to touch him. A smug smile played at the corner of Eli's lips.

"What do you say, Piper?" My father's voice was tart.

"Thank you." The words sound hollow.

"You weren't going to tell me that you lost your wallet or your calculator?"

"Sorry," I said. "I thought I'd find them."

"You thought you'd find them," he repeated, his voice mocking. "You owe Eli an apology."

So my father had weighed the two of us and decided I was the one who'd offended him. God.

You're a survivor, Piper. Be smart. Just say you're sorry and take your licks and fight another day...

It was getting harder with every day closer to my eighteenth birthday and my escape, but this was when I'd have to be the most careful.

Still, a lump lodged in my throat, and it was hard to form the words of an apology around it. I owed Eli something, but it's sure as hell wasn't an apology. One day he'd find himself getting exactly what he deserved. And I'd be the one who gave it to him, so help me God.

Eli's eyes met mine. There was victory in his gaze and in the way his lips turned up around the edges, even though he was trying to bite back his smile. He enjoyed my misery.

"Piper." My father's voice was full of warning.

"It's all right, Steve," Mr. Kingston said. "It was just a misunderstanding. Let the kids work it out."

My father's jaw set. Mr. Kingston was trying to help, but he was just making things worse by undermining my father's authority, and nothing was as precious to my father as his authority. Certainly, I'd never been anywhere near as precious.

I just have to get through this. I stared into Eli's eyes, hoping to communicate telepathically that no matter what I said now, I'd be his bloody end one day.

"I'm sorry," I said.

"For what?" My father's voice was low and dangerous. This was just getting worse. If I'd managed to apologize right away, if Mr. Kingston hadn't said anything, maybe this would be over already.

"For pushing you," I said to Eli. The memory rose quickly in my mind—Eli falling backward, about to land on his ass—and it was my turn to hide the impulse to smile. They could make me say 'I'm sorry,' but they couldn't change what happened.

"And for being rude," my father said. "If Eli still wants to go out with you, despite all your foolishness, I'll allow it. She'd be a lucky girl." He said that last to Mr. Kingston, who nodded.

"Thank you, sir," Eli said.

Shit. Shit. Shit.

"Piper and I can talk about it at school." Eli's lips turned up even more. The smug, self-satisfied, sick asshole.

"Sounds good," my father said briskly. "All right, well, my apologies again."

He was already swinging open the front door. As much as I didn't want Eli and Mr. Kingston to stay, I didn't feel exactly peachy about having them leave, either.

"Have a good night," Mr. Kingston said. "We're on for poker this weekend?"

"Of course," my father said.

He hosted every month. It was always a good night. Maddie and I watched movies in my room while his friends took over our basement. We weren't allowed downstairs, but he always got us a pizza and snacks. It was my favorite night every month, a bright spot that I looked forward to.

He nodded goodbye, and Eli and Mr. Kingston filed out the door. They headed across the long green lawn. Eli's black Hummer was parked on the street. Mr. Kingston must have let him drive. I still hadn't learned.

When my father closed the door, he stayed very still for a second, his back to me, his hand on the doorknob.

I waited, still as a rabbit, my heart pounding in my chest.

He closed the deadbolt and turned to me, the expression on his face thunderous.

"You embarrassed me, Piper," he said, his voice low. "Mr. Kingston is my friend. Eli is one of your oldest friends."

I didn't think either of us believed that was true.

"What's come over you?" he asked me.

"I'm sorry," I said, and even though I didn't mean it any more than I did before, the words fell easily from my lips.

His fingers crawled over the buckle of his belt. There was a soft whisper of leather as he pulled it out of his belt loops before it hung from one of his big fists.

Still, the belt wasn't the worst thing that'd ever happened to me.

"Get up to your room now," he told me.

4

My father kicked an empty laundry basket across the floor of my room.

I was putting all my stuffed animals into a trash bag, like he told me, and I was so thankful I was the one who dropped the nanny-cam bear into the black plastic bag. *Please, God, let me get this thing back.* Without it, I didn't know how I'd ever get custody of Maddie.

"You want to have an attitude?" my father told me, breathing heavily. "You can stop and think about how lucky you are to have everything I've given you. You don't have anything on your own, do you?"

"No," I said quietly. I jammed what used to be my favorite teddy bear into the bag, and its little face looked up at me as I tied the bag shut. They were just stuffed animals, and I was almost eighteen. It wasn't like I *needed* them. But this reminded me of all the other times he'd stripped my room when I was younger. I'd choked on my hot tears and my desperation, afraid I'd never get back the things that comforted me at night. Because all I had was *things;* I didn't have anyone.

Maddie had me, and I wasn't going to lose her. I'd never leave her feeling as lost and alone as I'd felt.

My eyes were hot, and I carried the bag down the long, sweeping stairs, through our foyer and the kitchen to the attached garage. It was quiet in the three-car garage, away from his anger, and I took a second to breathe. My heart still pounded wildly in my chest at the thought of fishing through the bag for the nanny-cam bear. I didn't want to risk him finding out what I was up to. I looked over my shoulder, irrationally afraid he was watching..

But this time, he was. He stood in the doorway, radiating anger, and he held out a thick, hard-backed, glossy book with two hands.

Fuck.

It was one of my textbooks, not something he'd usually take from me. I'd taped an envelope into the inside back cover. Whenever he sent me into a store with his debit card, I'd buy two of something, return one immediately after, and pocket the change.

"Where'd you get the money from, Piper?" he asked, his voice warning.

"I've been saving up," I said.

"Don't lie to me. Did you steal from me, or from someone else?"

"I had birthday money." I met his gaze steadily, letting him see my fear but trying to look innocent.

"There's eighty dollars here." His teeth were clenched, and he emphasized each word, like a bomb dropping between us.

"I get twenty dollars from Grandma every holiday."

"She doesn't send you twenty for President's Day, Piper, and that's the only way you'd have this much money saved up. If she sent you money every Monday you had off school." His voice was acerbic. "What else am I going to find in your room? Is there more?"

"No," I promised softly.

He reached into his pocket and drew out a hot pink pencil case, one I'd stashed in one of the bins that sat on my bookcase. My heart sank as he unzipped it and shook a handful of crumpled ones and fives into his hand. "How'd you get this?"

"Just change when I do our laundry," I said.

"Then it's my money," he said. "You're stealing from me."

"I didn't mean it like that," I said. "It was just change. Stuff no one would miss."

He closed the distance between us, and I caught one look at his face—his icy blue eyes, the tight fury etched in the lines around his eyes—and looked down, avoiding his gaze.

His voice was ice-cold, not hot like usual. "It's not *just change* to me. It's what it means, Piper. I can't trust you, can I?"

"I'm sorry," I started to say again, but his hands were already on my shoulders.

He shook me so hard my teeth rattled together, the world spinning. I tried to keep my balance, but he shoved me away, and I stumbled backward. I hit the side of the Lexus, catching myself with my hands against the smooth paint job.

His hand whipped across my face—the pop startling me more than it hurt—and then a second time, and then a third, and by then it did hurt, a lot. My ear popped and then sound faded for me, my father's voice suddenly soft. The fourth *smack* wasn't so loud, but my cheek burned and my teeth ached from slamming together.

He didn't usually hit me in the face—he needed for Maddie and me to look pretty and speak nicely and make him look good—but he was losing control.

And that was terrifying. He never meant to hurt me *badly*, but sometimes it happened anyway. One time, when I was a kid, he shoved me down the stairs, and I broke my arm. He'd been so furious at me that he'd refused to talk to me afterward, and it had only been hours after that he came and picked me up, cradling me against his chest, and put me gently in the backseat of the car for the ride to the hospital. And he'd told me what to say, and I'd said it.

Now, his fingers were in my hair, and I rose onto my tiptoes, trying to keep him from jerking out the roots as he dragged me across the garage. He pushed me against the side of his old Mustang—and a small crazy part of me thought, *did he really just relocate me to a cheaper automobile because he doesn't want to beat the shit out of me against the Lexus*—before his belt whipped against my thighs. I tried to push back, but his forearm dug into my shoulder blades, pinning me to the car. *Don't fight back, don't fight back. Just let it be over with.*

Then he was on top of me, shoving me to the ground, pinning me against the cold concrete floor. He sank all his muscular weight against me. He was so heavy I could barely draw a breath.

He hit me in the face, and the world turned red. I thrashed, getting an arm free, and struck out at him, but the hit didn't connect. I knew better than to fight back, but sometimes instinct took over.

Then suddenly the weight was off me. I scrambled to my feet, my vision clearing, although my ears hummed so loud that I could barely hear anything else.

My father was splayed across the metal shelves at the back of the garage as if he'd been flung there. Then suddenly he stumbled forward, falling to his knees. He caught himself, his hands taking the impact, and groaned.

When he looked up at me, his eyes were full of rage.

I ran for the door to the house and grabbed the keys that hung on the hook just inside by the kitchen cabinets, then slammed my shaking palm against the garage door button.

His eyes widened in understanding, and he started to climb to his feet, but he favored his knee and it took him a second as I ran to the front door of the Mustang, putting the car between us. He launched himself toward me, but he had to come around the trunk of the car, and I was already slamming the door shut, frantically hitting the lock button. His hand slammed into the window, making me jump. My hands shook as I stuck the car key into the ignition.

"Don't you do it," he said, warning me. He grabbed the door handle, and my breath caught in my chest, but the door didn't open.

The rolling door to the garage opened slowly. I tried to put the car into drive, but it wouldn't go. My father abruptly turned away, heading for the house. Fuck. There were spare car keys there, and he could also close the garage door on me. The brake! I had to put my foot on the brake. I did, yanking the car into drive, and the car rolled forward under the still-opening door. I thought I was going to hit the door, but the rattling door rose over the windshield, and then I was out. The car rolled slowly down the driveway to the dark street ahead.

My father came running out, chasing after me. I tried to focus on getting the car moving forward, my feet slipping on the brake and pedal, but I couldn't stop looking at the rearview mirror. He came to a stop, watching me go, and even from here I could see his eyes glittering with fury. I turned from our driveway onto the street, aware he'd gone back into the garage. Maybe he was giving up. Or maybe he was getting one of the other cars to follow me.

I hit the accelerator, and the car leaped forward. My fingers tightened on the steering wheel. My dad kept saying I wasn't ready to get my license, but I'd taken the school driving course, and he'd let me drive a few times. I knew the basics.

Still, if he called the cops, I was driving without a license. And had stolen his car.

But he probably wouldn't do that. He wouldn't want to air the family dirty laundry.

I reached a stoplight as I drove through town, and I glanced in the rearview mirror again, sure he'd be right behind me. He wasn't, but my face in the mirror caught my attention. My cheek and eye were swollen, beginning to bruise already. I looked awful. He wouldn't want anyone else to see me like this.

I rubbed my hand across my chest. My heart hammered so hard still that it hurt, and I had to calm down. I had to think. Maddie was safe. I didn't have to go home tonight, but where the hell was I going to go?

The light turned green, illuminating the quiet street. The grocery store was closed, but the 24-hour diner and the laundromat next door was still open. We lived in a quiet town, surrounded by country.

I had to go somewhere my father wouldn't find me. I checked the gas gauge. I had plenty of gas. Small mercies. A car rolled up behind me, and panic bubbled up in my chest again. But it wasn't one of my father's cars. They honked. Right. I lifted my foot off the brake and let the car roll through the intersection, then pumped on the gas. I'd head out of town and just drive the country roads for now. Eventually, maybe I could find a place to park and feel safe enough to fall asleep.

Or maybe I should go to the hospital. Maybe someone would help me. My lips twisted at the thought. I was so close to being old enough to live on my own, but I didn't think anyone was going to rescue my sister and me. My father was a powerful man. I figured if I had enough evidence, I could leave home and try to get custody of my sister. I wasn't going to run away and leave her there, and I wasn't going to see my sister lost in the foster care system. I could take care of us.

Tears blurred my eyes. If I could take care of us both, then why the hell was I so grateful she was somewhere else tonight? I was letting her down, and I didn't know how to do any better.

A dog streaked past the front of my car, a blur of white fur. I slammed on my brakes, which threw me up against my seatbelt. My car fishtailed.

The world outside the car revolved. Pine trees, empty road, pine trees again. I clutched the steering wheel for my life.

The car came to a stop. The world was deathly silent.

5

Oh my god, did I hit the dog?

I released my seatbelt and threw open the car door. The dome light turned on, illuminating a small stretch of the long country road. I looked back the way I'd come. Was he following me? I hadn't gotten that far after all. He might well find me here.

My heart rattled in my chest, telling me to get back into the car and drive away. He'd never mean to, but if he got his hands on me, my father might kill me tonight.

The headlights illuminated an empty stretch of the road in front of the car. I could have sworn the car slammed into something when it fishtailed, and I looked for a tell-tale dent. Then I walked in front of the car, still searching.

There was something white on the side of the road, in the bushes, and I ran toward it.

Bright eyes met mine in the dark. The next second, I could make out the figure in the darkness: the enormous white body of a dog, the bright green eyes. It stared at me, whining.

"Sorry boy," I said. "You're going to be all right."

I knelt just out of reach, afraid the dog would snap at me in its pain, but its bright, keen eyes seemed intelligent. It whined again, and I realized there was blood all over the white fur, as if he'd broken his back leg.

"I've got to get you to the vet," I said, and he whined louder. "Jeez. How am I going to do this?"

He was such a big dog. He might weigh damn near as much as I did.

"Hang on," I told him, before running back to the car. I leaned into the driver's side and popped open the trunk. My father was an abusive asshole, but he was also practically a Boy Scout in his preparedness. The trunk was always organized neatly with spare blankets, emergency flares, first aid equipment and bottled water. Sure enough, I found a stiff gray wool blanket. If I could wrap the dog up in it, I could hopefully help buffer myself in case he snapped when I tried to pick him up.

I returned to the dog, making comforting noises, and draped the blanket around his shoulders. He looked at me with a look of extreme doubtfulness written across his doggie face.

"Trust me," I said. "I know I don't seem that competent based on my driving skills, but I promise. I'm going to take care of you."

I tried to ease him into my arms, and he moaned.

"What the hell are you doing?" It was a boy's voice, rough and gravelly and familiar.

I almost dropped the dog as I looked up, shocked.

Kai stood at the edge of the road. His chest was heaving, as if he had been running. Since he wore nothing but jeans, I could see the way his chest fluttered with his breaths. He had powerful pecs and chiseled abs that were surprising for a high school boy. He raked his hand through his dark hair as he stared at me.

"You hit the dog," he said flatly.

"I didn't mean to."

"You hit *my* dog," he said, and the dog barked at him, as if he was irritated. "You keep turning up, don't you, Piper?"

"I didn't mean to hit your dog," I snapped. "It was definitely not on tonight's to-do list. Now we have to get him to a vet—will you help me move him?"

Kai came and stood next to me instead, then dropped to my side to examine the dog. His shoulder brushed mine. His naked skin felt hot to the touch, his muscle hard, and something in me stirred at the unthinking way his body brushed against mine. It was just practicality that brought him so close.

He looked his dog over, his movements quick and impatient, then gentle when he touched the dog's hindquarters.

"It's broken," he said.

"That's why I'm trying to get him to the vet," I said. "I could've told you that."

He shook his head. "Christ. This night just keeps getting better."

"I'm having a great night too," I promised him, irritated by his tone.

His gaze turned my way, and his eyes widened as they met mine. "What the hell happened to you? Were you hurt in the accident?"

"You've got a lot of questions," I shot back, mimicking his complaint earlier in the day.

He took my jaw in two fingers, his gaze steady on my face. My breath caught at his grip on my chin as he examined me. There was something so caring in the touch, even though he was so brusque and rude.

"That wasn't from the accident," he said decisively. His tone was raw and angry, and I felt a spike of fear before he suddenly released me. He jumped to his feet. "Come on. I'll get the dog into the car. It'll drive, won't it? You can drive us home."

"Yeah, I can drive. But home won't work. He needs a vet—"

"I can do better than a vet," he told me impatiently. "My uncle's a doctor. You going to take us or not?"

"Of course I'll take you." I'd do anything to undo what had happened tonight.

He leaned forward, scooping the dog into his arms. "Take it easy, *dog.*"

The dog whined louder, a keening sound that broke my heart, as he lifted it easily off the ground. The dog had to be well over a hundred pounds, but Kai carried it easily to the backseat of the car. I scrambled to open the car door for him, and he bundled the dog into the backseat. Then he slid into the seat too, as if I were their chauffeur. It was the least I could do after that, anyway.

I ducked into the seat and pulled the seatbelt across my lap. "Where am I going?"

"I'll tell you," he said.

I put the car into drive and carefully pulled onto the road. I glanced in the rearview mirror. Headlights were coming, in the far distance, and I slammed my foot down on the gas. The car leaped forward.

"Christ!" Kai said again.

"Sorry." I glanced in the rearview again, looking for the headlights, and met his eyes. They looked black in the dim light of the car, and he stared at my reflection knowingly.

"Since your car still drives just fine, why didn't you drive away?" he asked.

"I didn't know if the dog was okay," I said. "What's his name?"

"He doesn't have a name. He's a stupid mutt. I'm not sure we should keep him if he's going to run off like that." He rattled the words off, but his tone didn't quite sound genuine. His words were cruel, but it didn't seem like he meant them. Maybe I was giving him too much benefit of the doubt, though.

"He's beautiful," I said, thinking of the alert, intelligent face and the black-lined green eyes that stood in contrast to the gray-and-white fur.

Kai snorted. "If you like dogs so much, maybe you shouldn't hit them with your car."

I didn't bother to say it was an accident again. What if the dog wasn't okay? It hadn't been my fault, but that didn't take away the horror of that impact, or of the dog groaning, or the way the dog had looked at me for help, as if despite what I'd done, he believed I could help him. I bit down hard on my lower lip, trying to fight back the hot tears that flooded my eyes.

Kai leaned forward, his eyes wide with alarm, and for a second, it looked as if they were full of empathy. "Are you crying?"

"No," I lied, my voice coming out thick.

"Jesus, girl, you aren't good enough behind the wheel to cry and drive at the same time!" he said.

His blunt statement flipped my sadness over to anger, and when I blinked, those tears streaked down my cheeks. My gaze was clear again. "You are an ass, you know that?"

His lips quirked up sardonically. "I don't owe you anything, Piper. Not even nice. We don't know each other yet."

"I try to be nice to everyone," I said.

"How's that working out for you?"

His cold words hung in the air.

"Not that great, I guess," I said. "Since that's how I ended up meeting you."

At the insult, his lips widened, his smirk bordering on a genuine smile. "You should be careful who you're nice to. This world is full of wolves, and worse."

"Just because you're nice doesn't mean you can't take care of yourself," I told him.

"You don't look like you've been taking care of yourself, girl," he said. "Who did that to you?"

I shook my head.

"Tell me." A low, fierce edge found its way to his voice.

As if he cared. After the way he'd talked to me, so cutting and rude, he must just be recreationally curious. I wasn't going to shake out all my hurt and agony for his amusement.

"I don't owe you anything," I said, repeating his words.

He straightened up. For a second, his eyes met mine in the rearview again. He looked...wounded.

"You're right," he said. "You're going to turn left at the intersection. Then slow down...the turn into our property is easy to miss."

"All right."

"It's lonely out there," he said. "Not a lot of people know our place."

My father wouldn't find me there. Kai's words might have been chilling, another time, but right now it reminded me that I was safe.

I'd take my chances with the wolves of the world. The worst danger to me was in bright rooms and big houses.

"Do you mean to be creepy or does it just kind of come naturally?" I asked.

"You always this sassy?" He leaned forward again, pointing into the darkness to the left. "You better brake. You're going to miss it."

I slammed on my brakes and made a hard left.

I looked behind me, one last time, at the dark, empty road I was leaving behind.

The car bounced over a rough, unpaved driveway, a long track that wound through the woods, as I headed off toward god-knows-where.

6

I don't know what I expected at the end of the long dirt path, but it wasn't to emerge from the shadows of tangled trees to an open green lawn and an enormous stone house, almost a castle, flooded by moonlight.

I drove across the grass to park at the base of the porch steps. It was a sight, but I had no time to gawk.

Kai was already out of the car by the time I'd thrown open the driver's side door. He moved impossibly fast and with such grace, it was hard not to admire his muscular form despite his gruff personality.

He leaned in to pick up the dog with gentle care. He straightened with the dog in his arms, his biceps straining with the weight, veins standing out on his corded muscles.

"Welcome home," he said sardonically. "Get the front door."

I ran up the steps ahead of him, crossing the front porch—catching a quick glimpse of a porch swing and a chess board flanked by rocking chairs—to the front door. A fancy security key pad glowed next to the door, and I hesitated.

"The door," Kai said urgently. "Just get the door."

I tried the knob and it turned in my hand, so I pushed the door open. The expansive entryway was a blur of hardwood floors and deep red paint, and Kai rushed past me, down the hall.

"Callum!" he shouted. "Callum, we need you!"

Then he thundered down a flight of stairs to the left, leaving me alone in the hall.

"Okay," I said, taking a step back. Despite everything he'd said, he seemed frantic to get help for his dog. My instinct about Kai was he wasn't as much of a jerk as he seemed to be on the surface. But maybe that was wishful thinking.

I was alone now, in this big entryway flooded with moonlight. Somewhere off in the distance, a dog howled. After a second, another dog joined in, the two of them baying together. The primal noise made my arms prickle, goosebumps rising, and I rubbed my hands over my arms to warm myself.

I didn't belong here, and I should go back, get into my car, and drive away. A normal, smart girl would do that. I'd delivered the hurt dog to its people.

But it seemed safe here. I felt, deep in my bones, this was a place where I could get some rest, and I couldn't make myself walk back through that door and into the night.

From behind me, Josh said, "Piper?"

I turned to meet his gaze, and suddenly the room felt hot and bright. He stood just inside the entryway, wearing jeans and a black Northface fleece that clung to his broad pecs and the narrow taper of his waist.

Did I have a crush on Josh? I'd never looked at a guy before and had it seem as if there was a glow around him, never had the room turn so warm that my cheeks flushed. I should tell him why I was in his house. But I couldn't think of how to begin.

He swiped his hand through his hair, looking as lost as I felt. "What are you doing here?"

That was a crushing reminder that I shouldn't be.

"I'm in trouble," I said, which was true, too true, and inappropriate to blurt out. I tried to make myself smile into the divide between us as Josh's eyes widened. "I, ah, hit your dog. Kai's dog? Your dog? I'm so sorry."

"Kai's dog," he repeated, his brow furrowing. "All right. Where are they?"

"Kai took him downstairs."

"Come in the living room." He rested a big hand on my shoulder. "I'm going to go check on them. I'll be right back, okay?"

"He was looking for Callum," I said. His touch on my shoulder felt warm, almost feverish, but his hand itself was a comforting weight. There was something protective about his grip as he guided me into a room off the entryway.

It was another massive room, but it felt comfortable, with a huge wrap-around tan leather sectional, a crackling fireplace, and built-in shelves full of books.

"Piper," he said softly, frowning, as if he knew I was in real trouble. But he shook his head, as if he had something more pressing to take care of, then pushed gently down on my shoulder, encouraging me to take a seat on the couch. "One minute. That's all. Don't run off, okay?"

"I won't," I promised.

Just as Josh reached the doorway, a man burst in the front door. "You found him?"

"He's downstairs," Josh said quickly. The man who had just come in ran across the hallway, then rushed down the stairs.

Josh glanced back at me, his eyes full of worry, then shut the door between us.

Alone again, I scooted across the buttery-soft leather to sit at the end of the sectional closest to the fire. I was starting to shiver now, as if the adrenaline of the night had worn off. The shivers made my muscles ache. They were bone-deep and intense as if my body was trying to shake itself apart from within.

Normally, on a night that had gone sideways like this, I'd be locked in my room. I'd crawl between the fitted sheet and the bare mattress for a little bit of warmth, because that was all he'd left me. I'd shiver alone in my fancy princess' room that he'd stripped bare.

The only thing worse than being a monster's daughter is if that monster is king.

The door behind me opened. I knew it was Josh without looking back; I could feel the warm, commanding, confident nature of his presence. There was something magnetic about that boy.

"You're shaking," he said softly.

"It's cold," I said.

"Is that all it is?" He cocked his head to one side, studying me. Another shiver wracked through my body, my back aching faintly with the tightness of my cold muscles, and I leaned toward the fire.

He crossed the distance between us in a few quick strides, already pulling his fleece over his head. Each step revealed more of his body as he stripped off the fleece. One step, and he gripped the hem, raising it to reveal the defined squares of his chiseled abdominal muscles. Another step, and his elbows were even with his shoulders, revealing tattooed pecs. He had tattoos when he was just my age? Josh's easy smile and flirtatiousness had made me think he was clean-cut and easygoing, but now I wasn't sure. Another step, and his handsome square-jawed face disappeared into the fabric, his broad biceps defined in motion.

Then he held out his fleece to me. "Go on, take it."

"You're quite gallant." I hesitated. Kai had been running around shirtless, and now Josh, too. These boys seemed allergic to clothing.

Not that I was complaining.

"I am, so I'd be put out if you didn't humor me," he said, shaking the fleece at me. His gaze caught on the side of my face, as if he was studying the bruises, and his voice went gravelly when he ordered, "Take it."

I reached out to the fleece, and my fingers grazed his. Just touching him made me warmer, and I turned away, afraid my face would betray me, as I pulled his fleece over my head. It smelled like boy in the best kind of way, like pine and wood smoke and a faint, pleasant scent of fresh sweat, as well as crisp, clean aftershave. If he weren't standing right in front of me, gazing at me with that look of concern on his face, I would probably bunch the fleece to my nose and inhale.

Instead, I put it on quickly and fixed a smile on my face as I drew my hair out of the collar. "Thank you."

"Let's get you warmed up," he said, resting his hands on my upper arms. He rubbed them up and down briskly. "Are you going home tonight, Piper?"

The question surprised me. "Shouldn't I?"

"It's up to you," he said softly. "Depends on what happened to you."

"It's nothing," I said.

"Yeah, I've run into that kind of nothing before too." Something bleak flashed through his eyes before his characteristic smile came to his lips again.

I stumbled for something to say into the crackle of the air between us. "How's the dog?"

"The dog is fine." His lips twisted with the words, as if there was something funny. "Just a broken leg. No internal bleeding. He'll be right as rain soon."

"Where's Nick?" I asked. "Were you all out searching for him?"

"Yeah," he said. "Everyone should be heading back now. Are you hungry?"

He abruptly turned and headed for curtained French doors at the back of the living room.

My stomach growled faintly. "I guess so."

"Come on, Piper." He paused with his hand on the door, looking back at me. "I can't fix what's going on in your life. But if it won't make things worse, I can give you one night away."

"I don't think anything can make things worse than they are now." My father needed time to cool off. In the morning, there'd be hell to pay, but it would be survivable.

I didn't know why I'd just admitted that to Josh, though, who looked at me with sympathy. There was something about his gaze on my face that made it impossible to lie to him, as if he drew the words out of me.

"Then come on," he said, pushing open the door.

I followed him, reluctantly leaving the warmth of the fire. The thick rugs over the polished hardwood floors were soft underfoot, and I glanced at the leather-bound books that filled the shelves, suddenly realizing how ancient and rich their library looked. I was curious, but I was more curious about Josh.

He was a cute guy, sure, but there was something strange about the instant magnetism he held for me. He drew me to him. I didn't want to get back into my car and drive away from this house, but I also felt foolish, afraid that he'd notice I had a crush on a boy I met just today.

He led me into an enormous white-and-brass, eat-in kitchen with a table for six, and a row of dark wood stools at the long white granite island. He patted the island next to one of the stools, then continued around to stand at the gas stovetop. "What are you in the mood for?"

"What can you make?"

He grinned. "I can make almost anything. The fridge is fully stocked and I'm pretty amazing."

"Really?" I asked skeptically.

"What, you don't think I could be amazing?" His tone was teasing.

An image popped into my mind of Josh *being amazing* in an entirely different way—him standing behind me, his powerful arms caging me against the cool granite, as he rocked into me over and over. I bit my lip, as I imagined myself holding back a cry of bliss.

"I do think you could be amazing," I said, "but I guess I didn't expect culinary arts. I figured you'd be amazing at sports or something..."

"I do like to run." He came around the island to me, putting his hands on my shoulders gently and steering me toward the fridge. He pulled it open, and behind him were rows of clear plastic shelves filled with produce and cheese and gallons of milk. He knelt to look through the meat drawer. "Do you want steak? Chicken? I can make you fajitas or a burger or..."

"Stop showing off, Mr. Mom." Kai said from the doorway. He

lingered there, and when I turned back, there was a hungry look in his eyes. I wasn't sure it had anything to do with fajitas.

Josh rolled his eyes. "I'll make burgers. Piper looks like the kind of girl who likes red meat."

I slid onto a stool, resting my elbows on the granite as Josh pulled stuff out of the fridge and returned to the island with his muscular arms full.

"Mr. Mom, huh?" I asked as he took a long copper grill pan from underneath the island and set it across the burners.

"Without our parents, we all have to help out around here," Josh said. "Don't let Kai fool you. He's the king of laundry."

Kai pulled a rueful face. He settled on the stool next to me. His elbow brushed mine as he shifted, getting comfortable, and waves of heat radiated from his still half-naked body.

"You want to put a shirt on?" Josh asked him drily.

"You should put a shirt on," Kai said cheerfully. "Grease splatters."

"I'll be fine," Josh said. "I donated my fleece to Piper."

"I can tell. I can smell you on her." Kai's nostrils flared.

"You think the fleece being four sizes too big is a clue too?" Josh's tone was joking, but the look he flashed at Kai was warning.

"Did you ask Callum if it was okay for us to have company?" Kai asked.

"It's our house too." Josh's jaw set.

"Well, he's the...dad. Pretty much now."

Josh finished forming a burger patty and laid it in the grill pan with a sizzle.

"How long ago did your parents pass away?" I asked.

"Going right for the big questions, huh, girl?" Kai said.

"Kai, be nice," Josh chided. "You brought her here."

"I needed a ride."

"Thanks for your help," Josh said to me. He melted butter into a frying pan and split buns in two, nestling them in the browning butter. The smell of beef and butter filled the air, making my stomach rumble.

"Which was only necessary because she was driving like a bat out of hell down the road." Kai slid off the stool and headed to the fridge, returning with a jug of lemonade and three glasses. He poured a glass of lemonade and slid it in front of me. "What were you running from, Piper?"

I took a long sip of the cold, sweet lemonade, and then set it down on the island without answering.

"I don't think she wants to talk about it," Josh said. "And that's all right." He gave me an encouraging smile.

"Do you do all the smiling for both of you?" I asked, glancing from Josh to Kai. I hadn't seen Kai crack a smile yet.

"Don't mind Kai. He's a little confused about what makes a man tough," Josh said.

Kai's eyes narrowed. I had a funny feeling they were returning to a fight they'd had before.

"And you're a little confused about when to keep your mouth shut," Kai said, but without rancor.

"Make yourself useful and get the lettuce out of the fridge."

Kai rolled his eyes but returned to the fridge. I was a little bit surprised to see him listen to Josh. He leaned in, his back muscles rippling, and pulled out a head of iceberg lettuce. He washed it at the white ceramic farmhouse sink and then set it on the island with a thunk.

"Ketchup, mustard, mayo, all of the above?" Josh asked. When I nodded, he finished two burgers, set them side-by-side on a plate with a handful of potato chips, and slid them across the island to me.

"Two burgers? She's human, Josh." Kai said, his voice full of humor. "Girls don't eat like that."

I took a dainty bite of my burger, a bit too aware of the two of them looking at me. It made me think too much about chewing. Suddenly, I worried I looked silly when I ate.

Josh put together four more burgers, and Kai took a seat beside me. When Josh pushed the plate across to him, he leaned over his food, stuffing into his mouth like he was starving. His shoulder brushed mine again, and as I breathed in his scent, the warm, pleasant odor of his heated body, I felt the faintest throb between my thighs. What the hell was wrong with me? He wasn't even *nice*.

The burger was perfect, crunchy around the outside from the grill, tasting of char and rich beef, soft and tender on the inside. My stomach growled again, my mouth suddenly thick, and I went to town. Dainty bites be damned.

Josh's eyes widened over the top of his own burger. He swallowed, then glanced at Kai, his lips widening as if he were self-satisfied. Kai glanced at me and then shook his head, returning to his own burger.

"Never mind," Kai said, "you don't eat like a girl."

"He means it as a compliment," Josh said, shooting Kai a look. Still, I set the second burger down, only half-eaten.

"Kai doesn't seem like a big purveyor of compliments," I said.

"*Purveyor*," Josh repeated. "I bet you did well on the SATs."

"I did okay, not that it matters." My dad said I was too immature to go to college in the fall. The words stung like nothing else he'd said to me, and he'd said a mouthful. I wanted so badly to go off to college on my own and live in the dorms, to have the chance to knit together my own life.

But, maybe once I had a job and custody of Maddie, I'd be able to go back to school. It was a different life than anyone would have expected, given the privilege I came from. No one knew the man my father really was, though.

I could get out of there on my own. My father thought I needed his money and his blessing, and he wouldn't realize he was wrong until I was gone.

"Why doesn't it matter?" Kai asked.

I froze, then put a potato chip into my mouth, letting the salt melt on my tongue. I shrugged. "Not college material, I guess."

Kai stared at me, his lips parting, his deep brown eyes troubled.

"We should start off getting to know each other with easier questions." Josh rapped his knuckles on the kitchen island. "I know. We'll play two truths and a lie."

"I'm not playing a stupid game," Kai said.

"Fine, you just sit there and be quiet then," Josh said.

"I hope one of your truths explains why you all hate shirts so much," I said.

Kai bobbed his head, and for the first time, I saw a small grin cross his narrow lips.

Josh shook his head. "She's got jokes."

But the teasing look he flashed me was warm, and I felt more content on this stool, with these two strangers, with my belly full and the sound of their warm, boyish voices, than I had in a long time.

7

"You are such a bad liar!" Josh exclaimed. When I tried to argue with him, making a case for the 'lie' I'd just told, I found myself giggling instead. I was actually a pretty good liar—my father had made sure of that with his brutal discipline—but for some reason, I couldn't help smiling self-consciously whenever I tried to form a lie with Josh's ocean-blue eyes regarding me skeptically.

"You have a guest." A man stood in the doorway, his arms braced to either side of the frame. He was the man who'd run through the foyer before. He was older than Josh and Kai, maybe in his late twenties, and his dark hair was wet, as if he had just showered. He was even bigger than they were, too, with a powerful, muscular body, a grown man's body.

Kai glanced at Josh. For a second, a flash of uncertainty crossed Josh's face, but then it was gone, replaced by his usual easy confidence. "Callum, this is our friend Piper."

"You've got friends after one day at school?" Callum smiled, and the tension in the room eased. He crossed the room to me, holding out his hand. "You must be a special girl to have won them over already. Especially Kai."

"I'm not sure I'd call Kai *won over*," I said. His skin felt hard and calloused and scarred, and when he took my hand in his, I could have sworn his pulse thrumming his palm, setting my own pulse rocketing along with his.

"He doesn't even like us and we're his family," Callum said, glancing at Kai. "I heard him laughing. I'd call that *won over*."

Kai pulled a face before he hunched his broad shoulders, leaning over the island to hide his expression.

"Do you mind if Piper stays the night?" Josh asked.

Callum glanced at me, then at Josh, and his nostrils flared. "I guess I don't see why not. But tomorrow is a school day. I don't want you to be...distracted."

"I won't be," Josh promised. "We're going to watch a movie in my room."

Callum's eyebrows rose, but he said nothing. He knit his arms across his broad chest.

"Let's get out of here before he changes his mind," Josh stage-whispered dramatically. He offered me his hand, as if I needed help navigating the eighteen-inch drop to the floor. I took his hand anyway as I slid off my stool.

"Be good," Callum said, when we were almost all the way to the kitchen door.

"Always." Josh didn't look back.

I wasn't sure if it was Kai or Callum who snorted skeptically behind us. Maybe both of them.

"I'll sleep on the floor," Josh told me, resting his hand on my waist with careless possessiveness, as if we knew each other well already. "You can take my bed."

Common sense reared its ugly head, belatedly. "I can't. I shouldn't be sleeping over...we barely know each other."

We reached the quiet of the hallway, and he turned, bracing one hand to the side of my head. I wasn't pinned to the wall by his body—he held himself away from me—but his intense blue eyes gazing into mine held me still.

"Piper," he said. "I know you don't want to talk to me, and I respect that. But I'm not an idiot. I'm looking at your face..." His eyes were kind as they swept over the bruises on the side of my face, but there was something fierce about the way his jaw set. "So help me God, if you go back there tonight, I might just kill him."

His voice came out low and threaded with protective fury.

"You don't even know me," I said softly. "You shouldn't care that much."

"Don't tell me what I should care about." His lips hovered at my eye level, and some crazy, wild part of me wanted to reach out and take his jaw in my hands, hold him still and press my mouth against his.

"It's just crazy. You don't know if I'm a nice person." My lips quirked. "And you can't even tell right now if I'm pretty or not."

"I can tell," he promised, smiling ruefully. Was it his protectiveness, or just the curve of his lush lower lip above that chiseled jaw, that made me throb to press myself against him? "But it wouldn't matter. You deserve to be protected. Cared for."

His words were too sweet, and I shifted uncomfortably, but I couldn't pull away. "I can take care of myself."

His thumb skated across my split lip. It throbbed sweetly under his touch. I couldn't tell if his gentle probing made it hurt worse or less. His tentative touch lingered, as if he'd heal my wounds. If he could.

"No one can take care of themselves," he said softly. "We all need a family. Friends. There's nothing that matters more to our happiness than knowing we aren't alone."

I couldn't hide the cynical twist in my lips. I tried to be there for Maddie, but family? Friends? No one had ever been there for me. "What would make me happiest is to know I was independent."

He leaned even closer, his breath in my hair when he whispered, "I think you'll find that's the real lie, Piper. Even if you mean it now."

I put my hands on his shoulders, intending to push him away, but once my fingers met warm, hard muscle, I couldn't quite bear to.

"You are intense," I said, ducking my head to hide my smile. I had to defuse the tension between us, and the tension I felt myself, the restless desire to push him against the opposite wall and kiss him hard. What the hell was wrong with me?

He wrapped a strand of my hair around his fingers. "Is that a problem?"

"It's...unusual." My voice came out husky.

He tugged gently on the strand, sending pleasant tingles across my scalp, and pleasure raced through the ends of my hair down my spine. I almost moaned in response. "Don't you think humans could use a little more intensity? More love, more loyalty, more honor." His voice went soft. "Does anyone see you, needing help?"

"If they do, they're ignoring me," I said, my gaze falling to his chest. I shook my head. "It's not their problem. Like I said, I can take care of myself."

For a second, he was silent. I had to know what he was thinking. When my chin rose, there was a challenge in his vivid blue eyes.

"Well, I see you," he said, and he tucked the hair back behind my ear, the gesture quick and fond. He stepped back, suddenly, and I almost sagged as if I'd been released from the wall, even though he'd never held me in place. Cool air skated over my body. "And I don't intend to pretend otherwise."

He turned, heading for stairs at the back of the hallway. "Want to come see my room?"

I didn't quite trust myself to speak. My knees still felt weak. I followed him—of course I did—and when I glanced back over my shoulder, Kai had emerged from the kitchen and stood watching us.

"Are you coming?" I said softly, stopping to look at Kai.

"Do you want me to?" he asked, his voice rough. He shoved his hands into his pockets and shot me a cocky glare, as if he didn't want it to matter to him.

"Suit yourself," I said, starting to head toward the stairs, where Josh had paused, his hand on the bannister. But there was something lonely about the idea of Kai knocking around this vast house by himself, while Josh and I got to know each other better, and so I turned back. Kai's face was frozen, his jaw lifted, his face expressionless. Before I could lose my will, I said, "Yes."

"Yes, you want me around?" he asked, his voice sullen.

"Kai," Josh said impatiently, jerking his head toward the stairs. "You are one of us, even though you're a pain in the ass. Come on."

I'd love to have known where the tension came from between them, when they'd lived together for however long it had been since their parents died. But I had a feeling it'd take time to unwind their secrets, just as it'd take time for them to unwind mine.

Why did I feel so certain that we would, in time, come to know each other well?

Kai shook his head as if Josh annoyed him, but he followed us up the stairs anyway. Ahead of us was a long corridor, with what seemed like endless heavy polished dark-wood doors, all closed. Between the doors were works of art, and crossed swords hung periodically between the art.

"You guys just moved here?" I asked. "You move fast with the decorating."

I stopped at an arresting, but disturbing, painting. A cluster of wolves stood around a woman in a gown. Snow fell, and even though her bare shoulders must have left her chilled, she looked up rapturously toward the falling flakes. Some of the wolves lay at her feet, gazing at her with adoring eyes, and others paced around, some of them staring out of the portrait with their teeth bared. They all looked so lifelike that the snowy scene sent a chill down my arms.

"You can tell we don't pay an interior decorator," Kai said, humor in his voice for once. "Weird shit, huh? Our rooms are normal, though."

"Does Callum like wolves?" I asked.

Josh pushed open his bedroom door and cocked his head at me, inviting me in.

"Like?" Josh repeated. "I guess so. He collects old art and arms and armor. Kind of a family hobby, passed down from his father."

"His father. Your grandfather?"

Josh's lips widened. "Are you trying to figure us all out, princess? We aren't that complicated."

"You admit to being unusual," I teased, following him into his room.

"Not really," he said. "You're right, I like playing sports. And I like playing the guitar, too. And I love superhero movies. Pretty much your standard boy-next-door."

His room was neat. His brass-framed bed stood against one wall, and for some reason the brass scrollwork in the headboard made me imagine—just for one naughty second—handcuffs dangling from the scrollwork. Framed movie posters hung on the wall, each for a different superhero flick.

"You really are boring," I said, to make him laugh, and he did. "I guess I'm just the normal girl-next-door, too."

"Oh, so do you like jocks who like dumb movies and play you songs on their guitar?" Kai asked. He bounced onto Josh's bed, stretching out as if he owned it.

"Yes," I said.

"Are you ever in luck then," Kai dead-panned.

Meanwhile, Josh's grin widened as he opened up the big cherry-wood cabinet at the foot of his bed, revealing a flat screen television and stacks of DVDs. "What do you want to watch? Something funny or something with a dose of vengeful justice?"

"Are those the two movie categories?" I squinted at his stack of titles. All superhero movies or comedy flicks. I guessed that for Josh, those really were the two categories. "You have some secret desire for vengeance, Josh?"

"Who doesn't? I'm picking for you if you don't pick in three, two, one..."

Before long, the three of us were on the bed. I found myself lying between them, feeling the heat of their two bodies radiating so that I was finally, truly, deeply warmed. I felt nervous at first, but that gave way to ease as they joked, and then we all fell silent, watching the movie.

I woke up in darkness, with a blanket tucked over my body. For a second, my heart froze in my chest. Then I heard Josh's soft breathing. I turned over and found him sleeping on the floor, like he said he would, just to one side of my bed. Another soft exhale caught my attention, and I sat up. Kai slept between the foot of the bed and the cabinet. His arms were knit behind his head, making the hard shapes of his bicep stand out in sharp relief, even though he was asleep. These guys really must be athletes—I'd never seen boys so cut at such a young age. Even the most fit guys I knew, like Eli, still had a lot of boyishness to their lean frames.

Callum's body rose in my memory, its sheer power, his massive biceps and pecs and the hard-muscled thickness of his waist. There was still a leanness to Kai and Josh, but Callum was all grown up, all powerful and solid. His arms would seem like an irresistible shield around any woman he locked them around. I could almost feel what it would be like to be crushed against his body, held tightly, the daydream as strong as a memory.

I shook my head. I was losing it.

I was lucky that Josh and Kai had welcomed me into their little circle as randomly and easily as they had, choosing to be my friends, it seemed, based off nothing. But that was no reason to get lost in a fantasy world.

Tomorrow, I'd have the respite of school. Then I'd have to hope that my father was, as he usually was, in a forgiving mood when I returned home. He often pretended to forget anything had ever happened, although my stuff would stay in the garage until he suddenly, randomly, piled it in the doorway of my room—either because I was truly forgiven, or because we were having company.

Tomorrow, it was back to playing the plan.

But for tonight, I listened to the soft breathing of these two guys in the night, and my own breath stilled. My hands had tensed on the blankets, holding them tightly as I thought about my father's reaction, but now they relaxed. My body felt heavy, the comfortable mattress pressing up against me, and I fell into sleep.

8

The next morning, I woke to an empty room. Sunlight fell at a slant across the wooden floorboards, illuminating dust floating in the air in a gentle golden haze. I sat up, my head still heavy with sleep. I needed coffee. How long had they let me sleep? Would we be late for school? I rolled onto my elbow, looking across Josh's nightstand for a clock.

Along with a small brass clock, that looked as antique as the rest of their collection upstairs, there were a few framed photos. In one, a toddler-version of Josh stood between two people who must have been his parents. Even though he was round-cheeked and tiny, there was no missing his trademark grin. His mother had windswept blond hair and a square-jawed, generous smile that was just like Josh's. His father leaned in toward the camera, and although his dark eyes and heavy beard made him look intense, his smile seemed to give away a good natured heart.

In another picture, Josh, Nick and Kai stood with their arms draped over each other's shoulders in the midst of the forest. Kai stood at the end, unsmiling, his eyes intent on the photographer. *Callum, it must have been Callum.* The other three of them beamed out of the photo.

I wondered why Kai was the way he was. Josh had implied he'd seen some rough times in his life, too, but he had such an easy, comfortable way about him still. Josh seemed like he tried hard to see the bright side in life.

But then there was that edge, beneath the charm and ease, when his voice had gone all fierce and rough. When he'd threatened to kill my father for hurting me. The thought made my chest squeeze. Josh would get himself into trouble if he tried to go against my father. I should have said that; I should have warned him. Instead, I'd been so lost in his gaze that I'd forgotten myself.

Feeling guilty, I slipped out of bed. The room was warm, surprisingly so, and I realized there was a small fire burning in the fireplace in the corner. This house was a maze of rooms and fireplaces. I wondered how long ago it had been built.

Just then, the door opened, and Josh came in. He handed me a cup of coffee. "I guessed at how you like your coffee."

I took a sip. "Close enough."

"Hot and sweet?" he said.

"Yeah, and I usually take milk, but I won't complain." The mix of bitterness and sweetness went down easily, warming my chest. "Did you start the fire for me, too?"

"Guilty," he said, leaning down to poke at the burning log with a metal stick. "I don't usually bother. I tend to run hot."

"I noticed." It was only once the words were out that I realized just seconds before, we'd discussed my affinity for things that were hot and sweet. Certainly, there were few people on the face of the planet as hot and sweet all at once as Josh.

He hung the poker back on a nail alongside the fireplace and sat down on the bed, tucking his leg beneath him. "I have to go to school today. I tried to get Callum to let me play hooky, but..." he shrugged.

"Callum takes his stand-in dad role seriously?" I filled in lightly.

"I just thought maybe you wouldn't want to go back." He cocked his head to one side. "I don't think school will be easy on you today."

"I like school well enough," I said, before thinking of Eli haunting the halls, staring after me with that hungry expression like he was wanted to eat me up. A shiver ran down my spine.

"Anything you want to tell me about?" Josh asked, his tone still easy, before he took a long sip of his coffee. His throat worked as the coffee slid down, and my eyes couldn't help following the shape of his jaw and neck.

I shook my head.

"Do you have enemies, Piper?" Josh asked.

"Enemies?" I smiled. "That's more archaic than your clock. Who has *enemies*?"

He picked up the clock in one hand, hefting its weight. "It was my grandfather's." His deep blue gaze swiveled back to me. "And who doesn't have enemies? Anyone who tries to do something with their life runs into people who can't abide them."

"I haven't tried to do anything with my life."

"Bad liar, again."

"You think too much of me, Josh." I shook my head. "You're going to be disappointed."

"Never," he said.

"You don't even know me."

"I've put together a few things about you already." He took another sip of his coffee, leaving me in suspense, but his eyes were still on me. I sat down on the edge of the bed, eying him. I was curious what he would say, probably more curious than I should be. I wrapped my hands around my mug and mimicked him, watching him over the top as he watched me.

"Are you going to enlighten me?" I finally asked him mischievously.

"Sure," he said, as if he'd just been waiting for me to ask, and raised his hand to tick things off on his fingers. "One, you're pretty all the time, but you're drop-dead gorgeous when you smile."

I bit my lip, shaking my head. I should say thank you, but his matter-of-fact compliment left me embarrassed.

And delighted, too.

"*That* face is pretty cute too," he told me. "Two, you're fun. I could have stayed up all night talking to you."

Instead, he'd let me fall asleep in his bed while he slept on the floor. Part of me had worried I was being stupid last night when I slept in his bed. Now I knew I'd never had anything to fear from him.

"And last of all," he said, "you were running from something, something that scared you bad, and when you hit something in the road, you stopped to check. You're both brave and kind."

Color rose in my cheeks. "I knew I'd seen a dog—"

"It doesn't make it any less unusual," he said. "Lots of people wouldn't stop for just a dog."

The way he looked at me, like I was something incredible, when I was so used to being looked at like I was nothing, made me uncomfortable. My gaze dropped.

"Let's go downstairs," he said. "Callum's making us all breakfast before school."

"That does seem very Mr. Mom."

"It's the least he can do for me right now," he said, an edge of bitterness in his voice. Then he shrugged, as if he were shrugging his feelings away. I wondered what bothered him. The tension between him and Kai seemed intense. I guessed things were complicated with him and Callum as well. How long ago did their makeshift family come together? When he talked about having been hurt, like I'd been hurt, I wondered if it had been Callum who did something to him.

He held his hand out to me as he opened his door, and when I walked out ahead of me, he touched the small of my back as if he was guiding me. His hand lingering on my back, just for a second, sent sparks flying up my spine. It wasn't just that his touch was full of heat and excitement for me; he touched me like I meant something to him.

Could he have the same kind of sudden, hopeless, crazy crush on me that I had on him?

Despite everything going on in my life, I felt a sudden rise of joy in my chest. I tried to push it down, though. A crush wasn't real.

My plan, my escape, my future independence—that was real. That was a lifeline.

No crush was going to solve my problems.

Downstairs, the kitchen was full of warmth and chatter. Kai and Nick both sat at the kitchen table, bantering with Callum. The aroma of bacon and coffee and the warm vanilla scent of pancakes hung in the air.

Today, everyone wore a shirt. That was notable. Unfortunate, but notable.

Nick's eyes widened as he saw me, and then his face brightened. Kai twisted in his seat, and he had the opposite reaction, falling silent.

Only Callum, who stood at the kitchen island, seemed unaffected. "Good morning, sleeping beauty," he said. "How do you like your eggs?"

"Oh, you don't have to make me anything special," I said. "I usually skip breakfast."

"Not in this house," Callum said. "It's the most important meal of the day."

"We've got to get to school soon," Josh said, casting a glance at the clock. "Or you know, not at all."

"School's important," Nick said, then grinned as Josh, who was in the process of sitting down beside him, threw an elbow his way.

"Only one day in and you already want to take a day off?" I asked lightly.

"I can't wait for the weekend," Josh said.

Kai patted the back of the chair next to him. "Come on, Piper. Let's see if you put away pancakes like you put away burgers."

"Kai," Callum said. "Be a gentleman."

Kai rolled his eyes. "It's like you don't know me at all."

Before I could sit, Callum slid a plate of crispy bacon across the island and glanced at me. "Can you put this on the table, please?"

As I reached the island, he leaned against the other side, resting his broad forearms on the granite. "I noticed your car is a bit dented up after last night."

It wasn't my car. And my father was not going to react well to the damage I'd done to the Mustang.

"Yeah," I said dully.

"I know a good body shop guy. He's quick and he owes me a favor," he says. "If you want, Josh could drive you and I could get your car in. I'll get it back to you after school."

"That would be…" I trailed off. "I can't. I can't pay for that."

"I'm not asking you to." His eyes flickered to the table, so quick it was almost imperceptible, before he looked back toward me. "That accident was our fault. We can take care of it."

I chewed my lower lip, and he said, "I insist, Piper."

His tone was firm but gentle. His deep, gold-flecked brown eyes met mine across the island. An inappropriate flutter rose in my chest, followed by warmth in my cheeks. He had to be ten years older than I was. He had graduated medical school, and here I was on the verge of dropping out of high school to run away. I must just seem like an awkward kid to him. Certainly, there was nothing but warm compassion in his eyes when he looked at me.

"All right, thank you," I said. "I'll give you my keys before we go."

"Good," he said.

I took the plate of bacon, feeling strangely self-conscious around Callum, and carried it to the table. I settled in next to Kai, wrapping my hands around my warm mug.

Callum settled a plate full of fluffy scrambled eggs and a golden-brown pancake in front of me. "You'd better throw some elbows if you want bacon. Kai usually tries to eat it all."

"Thank you." I smiled up at him.

"Next time, tell me how you like your eggs cooked," he said, heading back for the island.

"There's going to be a next time?" Josh asked, with innocent mischievousness, his eyebrows rising.

"Piper's your friend," Callum said, with subtle emphasis on *friend*. "It's possible. If Kai's manners don't scare her off."

Kai made a show of swiping a handful of bacon, then dropped the crisp, fragrant strips on my plate. "Eat up, hungry girl."

"Be nice to me," I said, but I picked up one of the strips of bacon and crunched into it anyway.

"We talked about *nice* last night." Kai's tone was mischievous, instead of rude, at least. He took a long sip from his coffee. The movement pulled the sleeve of his t-shirt up his arm, exposing the width of his bicep and the edge of a black tattoo I'd barely registered last night. I couldn't help being curious now about his tattoos, and Josh's, too.

"Sorry for the trouble with your car and everything," Nick said to me, drawing my attention. When I met his vivid green eyes, he was frowning, his gaze intense under his dark brows.

"It's okay." I couldn't tell now if it was my fault or not. Maybe I should have been driving slower. But just thinking about how I'd felt last night made my chest tighten, my heart beginning to race again. I tried to smile, but Nick's eyes widened, as if he noticed my reaction.

Nick reached across the table, leaning forward as if to comfort me, and his fingertips grazed my forearm. As soon as he shifted forward, he seemed to wince, biting down on his lower lip, as if the spontaneous movement had hurt him. I stared back, more confused about why he was in pain then I was about his touch, but he pulled back almost as quickly as he'd reached for me. Faint color rose in his tanned cheeks.

I stumbled for something to say, to ease the moment so he wouldn't feel self-conscious.

Josh said, "We should get to school." He clapped Kai on the shoulder as he stood from the table.

I shoved another, last piece of bacon into my mouth. It was only then that I realized that I felt *better*. All the anxiety, the constant low thrum of fear, the tightness in my chest and restlessness in my body, it had all faded away. I felt a warm sense of well-being instead. It was the same way I felt when I spent the day outside, as if I was grounded by nature.

Nick stayed at the table, unmoving, as Josh and Kai got up and headed for the hall. I pushed in my chair and then paused with my hands still on the chair back. "Aren't you coming?"

I felt the pause in the room, Callum and Josh and Kai listening for Nick's answer.

"I'm not feeling well," he said. "I'll be back in school soon."

It had the ring of a lie, and I frowned.

"You won't miss him," Josh said, joining my side. "He barely talks anyway."

"Be nice to your brother," I chided.

"Yes, ma'am," Josh said easily.

"It's actually a nice contrast with these two," Callum said, and Josh shook his head in response.

"See you later," I said to Nick, and he nodded back to me instead of saying anything. I glanced back into the kitchen when we reached the hall. He stayed still at the table as if he was waiting for something.

I didn't get a bad feeling from the four of them, but I definitely got a *weird* feeling. Something else was going on in this house.

I found my keys where I'd left them on the living room coffee table. Callum held his hand out. His forearms were marked with tattoos, more ink than Josh or Kai, but what drew my attention was his palm; it was covered with a spiderweb of raised white scars. I glanced up at his face quickly, embarrassed at having noticed, but still feeling a rise of curiosity.

He closed his fingers around the keys and thrust his hand into his jeans pocket, flashing me a casual smile. "See you after school. I'll bring your car."

"Not to my house," I said quickly.

"I'll bring it to you at school," he promised. "I'll be outside."

"You're a lifesaver," I said.

He nodded, but there was some quick flicker of emotion across his coolly neutral face that made me think he knew how much truth was in that sentence. My cheeks flared with heat—karma for making Nick blush, I supposed, even though I hadn't meant to—and I turned away quickly.

Josh stood in the door, holding it open for me. Kai was already past him on the porch, with a markedly patient, longsuffering look written across his face.

I was following the two of them across the yard to the car when I heard Nick's low voice, muffled by distance.

"We're just going to let her go home?" he asked. "To whatever's going on there?"

I couldn't see Nick when I glanced back, but Callum stood framed in the doorway, watching us go.

I had always had good hearing, better than anyone else I knew. Maybe it was a survival skill.

"Don't get distracted by the pretty face," Callum said, turning his back on the three of us. "We've got work to do here."

"It's not the *pretty face* bothering anyone, and you know it. If we don't get *distracted* by shit like that, are we really the good guys anymore?"

"Nick." Callum's voice was chiding.

Josh opened the passenger door for me, with a flourish, drawing my attention back to him.

Kai stared at me, a troubled look written across his face, as if he'd caught me eavesdropping. I stared back at him. Kai was far too observant for his own good, or mine.

I slid into the passenger seat, flashing Josh a distracted smile. "Gallant."

He winked at me, then closed the door. For a second, as he walked around the front of the car, I was alone with my thoughts.

What the hell was their *work*? What were they doing in our tiny town of Blissford, with their big house and their mysterious plans?

I had trouble enough of my own. I shouldn't worry about it. I should stay away from them.

Kai slid into the seat behind me. He leaned forward between the seats, as if he wanted to say something, but then he paused.

"What is it, Kai?" I asked, expecting the latest dig.

He seemed to consider his options. From my peripheral vision, I saw him lick his lower lip. He didn't seem like the type to hold back when he had something to say.

At least, I hoped he hadn't been holding back last night. I hoped that was Kai at his worst, because otherwise…my god. The boy had a sharp tongue.

Josh swung into the car beside me, his big shoulder briefly brushing mine, and I inhaled the scent of his aftershave and felt the heat coming off his body. The memory rose again of how he'd brushed his thumb over my lip the night before, the way the heat of his body had radiated against mine as he pinned me—sweetly—against the wall. Just the thought caused a sudden, strange throb low in my belly.

Whatever Kai had wanted to say, it was lost now. He leaned back. I caught his movement in the rearview mirror, and my gaze was drawn as he pulled his seatbelt across his chest. His gaze flickered up and caught me, our eyes meeting in the mirror for one charged second. Then I glanced away, out at the trees that lined the long driveway and hid the house from the road. They were beginning to change color now. Winter was coming on fast.

"Long driveway," I said as Josh put the car into drive, and we began to roll down the dirt track. "You guys like your privacy."

"You have your secrets too, Piper," Josh said lightly.

Well. He just cut to what I *really* meant. It was weird to have someone be so honest.

"Maybe," I said.

They didn't feel like secrets. They felt like chains, tying me to my father's house.

But one day—if I just stuck to the plan, if I didn't get distracted myself—my secrets were going to turn into the keys, and I would escape.

9

"Do you need to go home for your books and stuff?" Josh asked as we turned onto the long country road.

The thought made my stomach tighten, but my father would be at work already if this was a normal day for him. I doubted he'd stayed up all night, worrying about where I was and if I was safe.

"I don't want to make you late," I said.

Kai snorted. "You don't need to worry about us. A tardy is not really something I care about."

"Where do you live?" Josh drummed the wheel with his fingertips.

"Right outside of town. I'll show you." For some reason, it felt strange to bring them to my door. I'd met them less than twenty four hours before. Now they would know where I lived.

I thought of Josh, threatening whoever hurt me the night before, and I shifted in my seat. "If you'll stay in the car."

Josh's eyes flickered to the rearview mirror, exchanging a quick look with Kai I couldn't quite catch.

"All right." Josh said.

"No trouble," I warned.

Kai's lips turned up slightly. "No trouble, of course. My middle name is practically *no trouble.*"

"I doubt that very much."

We fell into comfortable talk about nothing important as I directed Josh toward my house. The guys had a lot of questions about school, and they laughed at my explanations of the strange characters dominating Blissford High, which encouraged me to tell them more.

The comfort fell away, though, when I had to point to my street. "This right."

Josh turned the wheel, his hands quick and competent, but he was suddenly quiet and unsmiling, to match my mood. We drove down the stretch of big homes, all set on rolling five acre lots. This was the nice part of Blissford: stone or brick homes, large and solid, set so far apart from each other no one could hear you screaming.

"This driveway," I said, my stomach tight, pointing to the pressed-concrete driveway marked by white stone pillars.

Josh turned, and we drove slowly up toward the stone house, an enormous block of a house in the midst of an expanse of green lawn.

There were no cars in the driveway, and the three white carriage-house style garage doors were all closed. The windows of the house were like blank empty eyes, staring out at us. There were no hints as to whether my father was truly gone or whether he was home this time.

Getting him back his Mustang unharmed would help us both pretend that nothing had happened. Showing up in a strange car with strange boys? That would not be helpful.

I fixed a smile on my face anyway as I opened the car door. "Be right back!"

Kai and Josh looked at each other, sharing some wordless communication. I shut the car door, the sound loud in the deep silence of the morning.

When I let myself into the house, it was quiet. I looked around the entryway—the ghosts of Eli and my father rising around me, the situation from the night before beginning to replay—and then raced upstairs.

With my heart pounding in my chest, I grabbed my books from the desk and threw them into my backpack. My room, with the stripped mattress and the bare shelves beneath the sparkly crystal chandelier, was a blur.

I hurried back down the stairs, stopping at the kitchen to grab a granola bar and an apple since I didn't see my wallet. My father must have taken my wallet and phone again. I threw them into the front pocket, zipping my bag up as I headed for the door. Maybe Josh and Kai would invite me to have lunch with them again. The thought made longing rise for me. I would like to sit in the cool air outside with them, having a break from the noise and chaos of Blissford High, but I didn't want to invite myself.

When I come back out the front door, the two guys leaned against the hood of the car, watching the house. Their arms were crossed over their muscular chests, and they looked protective. Warmth flooded my chest. There was just something about the way they seemed to want to look after me.

But I couldn't count on it. We barely knew each other. They were, as Nick had said, *nice guys*. That didn't mean they wanted to be with me. It just meant they didn't want to see anyone get hurt.

"I told you to stay in the car," I teased, tossing my backpack into the passenger seat and then swinging in myself. The guys both got back into the car too.

"You're not the boss of me, woman," Josh said, his voice light and teasing. "I stayed *by* the car. Close enough."

"Anyone home?" Kai asked.

I shook my head. I could just imagine the nightmare if my father had been in there, and if the guys had come in to rescue me... I knotted my hands in my laps. My legs were shaking, and I dug my fists into my thighs, trying to hold them still. I didn't think Josh or Kai missed much, and humiliation dulled my mind as they tried to make small talk again. This time, I didn't manage to be fun, and it bothered me. I liked that Josh thought I was fun.

A few minutes later, when we got out of the car in the student parking lot, I said, "Well, see you guys later."

Josh raised his eyebrows at me over the top of the car. "We're going to the same *room*."

"It's a small town," I said frankly.

He stared back at me. "And?"

"If you walk from here to there with me, people are going to notice." I gestured between the car and the school. "And they're going to say something about it. Maybe not something you hear, but they'll say something."

Josh rolled his eyes. "Well, let them say something, then."

"I'm just saying. Nothing's simple in a small town."

Josh came around the car to me, tossing his keys in his hand once before he slipped them into his pocket. "You don't have to make things complicated just because everyone else does, either."

"I don't mind," I said lightly. "I'm trying to protect your reputation. You're the new guys in school, and I am not the coolest."

Kai settled his hand on my shoulder, his fingers warm and solid, a comforting weight. "Have you even met Josh? He is not the coolest."

Josh grinned, a quick flash that made me want to smile too. "True," he admitted. "But we aren't going to tell anyone that. I'm going to win over this school by the end of the week."

"Cocky," I accused him.

"Bet me," he said.

"Bet you what?"

He shrugged. "We'll come up with stakes later."

"That sounds dangerous."

"Well." He started toward school, then glanced back at me over his shoulder, looking mischievous. "You aren't chicken, are you, Piper?"

"I'm not chicken." My tone came out offended—which was ridiculous—and the boys both grinned in response. "I just make good choices."

"Don't hang out with us then." Kai squeezed my shoulder briefly and then began to lope toward the school, passing Josh.

I hesitated, debating letting them leave me behind. For their own sake.

Josh put his hands to his chest and flapped his elbows, subtly, just once.

"I'll take your bet," I said, hurrying to catch up to them. "But you're going to end up regretting giving me undefined stakes when you lose."

"You might be surprised," he said. "I can be very charming."

"You should try it with me sometime."

He pulled a face, sticking his tongue out between his perfect white teeth, then threw his arm casually around my shoulders, tugging me into his side. Even when that boy made a face, it was adorable. It wasn't fair.

"Focus, you two," Kai said, looking hard at Josh. "We're at school now. Head in the game."

"I'm always focused," Josh said. "I can think about more than one thing at a time."

"You can barely think about one thing," Kai shot back. As the three of us walked up the stairs to school together, Kai sped up, pulling ahead of us like he couldn't stand the way Josh and I were touching.

Eli leaned against one of the doors into school, talking to his friends, and he eyed me hard as we walked toward him. Josh's arm dropped off my shoulder. He pulled himself to his full—considerable—height, although he didn't betray the slightest bit of tension.

Suddenly, Kai's pace slowed, and he was next to me again. His hands hung loose by his sides.

The three of us walked into the warmth of the hallway, leaving Eli's cold stare behind.

Kai turned around and, as he walked backward, he winked at me. "Stay out of trouble, will you?"

His wink would be on my mind all day. It was such an obvious, casual attempt to comfort me after Eli's death stare. And it was sexy as hell, too.

"I'll try. See you at lunch?"

He shrugged, his face shifting back to neutral, non-committal but gorgeous Kai blankness; his usual. "Maybe."

That *maybe* left me feeling more deflated than I should have, but I raised my hand in a quick wave before he turned and vanished into the crowd.

"That guy's Eli, right?" Josh asked, his voice false-casual. "Did you have a thing?"

"He thinks so," I said flatly. "He thinks we're still *having* a thing."

"He's bothering you?"

I shrugged. "You don't need to worry about it."

"If it worries you, it worries me," he said, his voice low and gravelly, the way it had gone when he touched the bruises on my face the night before. Then, as if he'd embarrassed himself, he shrugged, almost mimicking me a moment before.

If I'd felt like laughing, there would have been something funny about two people trying so hard not to care.

When we got into homeroom and took our seats, Misty leaned into the aisle, her eyes meeting mine briefly, a smile on her face. I smiled back. Then she looked over me, her gaze clearly fixed on Josh instead.

"Are you still coming to spirit night at Freddy's?" she asked him lightly. "Best burgers in town."

I was pretty sure that last night, I'd had the best burger in town. I'd definitely had the best view in town, given the guys' reluctance to wear shirts. I rested my elbow on the desk, trying to look casual. Like I was *thinking*, not eavesdropping.

I was totally eavesdropping.

"I wouldn't miss it," Josh said easily. "Maybe around seven."

"Maybe I'll see you there."

"Maybe."

Misty smiled at him and then swiveled back in her seat. The tips of her long brown hair whipped across my desk.

The flirtatious note in their voices did not make it sound like a *maybe*.

I crossed my legs at the knee, feeling restless and irritated. Misty's hair kept swirling across my desk, making it feel like her stupid head was far too close to mine. She must have washed her hair this morning; she smelled like strawberries and creamy lotion.

I probably smelled like bacon and black coffee, and whatever car accidents and heartbreak smelled like.

If I were a boy, I'd prefer Misty too.

When homeroom was over and the bell rang, Josh said softly, behind me, "Piper."

I pretended I didn't hear him, just for a second while I was throwing my backpack over my shoulder and debating what to say.

Then I turned back, smiling at him. What the hell. I met him *yesterday*. It was stupid of me to feel hurt if he smiled at another girl and used that same tone of voice with her he did with me. I had no right to feel possessive.

"Come on, Josh, let's get to Trig." Misty put her hand on his forearm, tugging him past me. I breathed in the scent of his aftershave as his eyes flickered to mine apologetically. Then the two of them were gone in the shuffle of humanity.

Everything was fine.

10

At lunch time, I headed outside, hoping—let's be honest—that Josh and Kai would have once again invaded my private lunch spot. As I crossed the green yard, I spied them far sooner than I should, though.

Kai and Josh sat at the same table as Eli and Misty and a few other popular kids. As I marched by them, a tingling sensation ran up my spine, as if someone was watching me. I lifted my chin up, but tried not to watch them back. My hips swayed awkwardly, like I'd forgotten how to walk.

It felt like an achievement to finally reach the tree where I usually hung out. Usually, I enjoyed the quiet. I put the tree trunk between me and my old—and new—friends. I sank to the ground cross-legged, shivering a little, and leaned against the rough bark. I pulled out my apple and crunched into it, and although it was sweet and juicy, I barely tasted it.

Everything was fine.

Even from here, I could hear them, though; the breeze blew their voices to me. Josh told a story that made everyone laugh, but Kai's occasional, sarcastic asides may have drawn more laughter. When the breeze suddenly died, I wished I could eavesdrop more.

I heard them all get up after a while and head back toward the school. The bell rang, distantly, and I wrapped my apple core in a paper towel and stuck it into the front pouch of my backpack. I should get back to school myself, but I didn't want to walk back in at the same time they did.

"Hey." It was Kai who suddenly stood next to me. Despite the black motorcycle boots he wore, he'd moved near-silently to join me. He sat, quick and graceful, and his shoulder brushed my arm.

"Hey," I said. "The bell just rang."

"Told you, I don't care about tardies." He bit down on a toothpick, which bobbed up and down between his teeth for a second as he chewed on it.

"You don't seem like you care about school much."

He shrugged, the movement making his broadly muscled bicep move up and down against my arm. "Should I?"

"I guess it depends on why you're here."

"I'm here because I have to be," he said lightly. "Like most kids."

"You don't seem like a kid."

His eyes flickered toward mine, widening just slightly—almost imperceptibly—before he glanced back out at the line of trees separating the school from the houses behind it. "Well, you don't either."

A sudden warm glow rose in my chest, and I turned away from him too, hoping none of it showed in my face.

"I guess neither of us should. Graduation's not that far away," I said lightly.

"Ehh." He leaned his head back, his eyes drifting shut. His dark lashes rested above angled cheekbones. "*Lots* of kids here. Worrying about kid stuff. Like fucking spirit night and who's going with who. And football practice and Friday nights—who cares?"

My cheeks warmed, but at least he wasn't looking.

"None of it really matters in the long run," I agreed. My long-run plan started to race through my mind once again: my birthday, my tapes, my request for custody of Maddie. I'd move us to the next city over, away from my dad, get a job, get an apartment. It wouldn't be easy, but I was someone who could do hard things. There were lots of things I didn't like about myself, but I was pretty sure about that.

I could do hard things, for Maddie.

Kai fell silent. He ran his fingers through his hair and glanced at me, then glanced away again.

"You don't talk much, do you?" I asked, thinking about how earlier in the car, he'd seemed on the verge of telling me something.

"You met Josh," he said. "I usually don't get much chance."

"It's just you and me right now."

"It is," he said, his voice warm.

I looked toward him, surprised by the note in his voice. His gaze met mine evenly.

"You're friends with Misty?" he asked.

Disappointment fell over me, hard, but I said, "Not really. We used to be friends."

"Why'd you stop?"

Misty had been my best friend when I was little. Her house used to be a refuge for me. "Grew up, I guess. Grew apart. We were born in the same hospital, almost the same day."

"Misty was born in the hospital here?"

"Yeah," I said. "Like...most babies. Where were you born? A barn?"

"You would think, huh?"

"I didn't mean..."

He shook his head. "Don't worry, you didn't hurt my feelings."

I blew out a slow breath, staring out at the trees again myself. Leaves rustled against each other in the breeze. I was so awkward; I should get away from Kai before I embarrassed myself anymore. "We should go into school."

"We should," he agreed.

Neither of us moved.

"Piper?" he asked.

"Yeah?"

He shook his head. "That name doesn't seem right for you."

"I didn't get to choose it."

"What would you choose if you were picking your own name?"

I was silent, thinking. For the first time, it occurred to me that maybe when Maddie and I started over, we should start with new names. It would help make sure our father couldn't find us again. But most of all, it would be a truly fresh start.

Our father couldn't choose who we were or who we became, even though he thought he could decide everything about our lives. He was going to discover how wrong he was.

"Would you be Kai, if you got to choose?" I asked.

"No fair turning the question around until you answer," he said.

"I don't know. You pick a name for me if you think Piper doesn't suit me."

"Piper just sounds so light-hearted," he said frankly. "And you seem to carry a weight. A burden. You carry it well, don't get me wrong..."

"I don't intend to carry it for long," I muttered, and Kai's eyebrows lifted curiously. I smiled, trying to pretend I hadn't given so much away. I had to distract him with something ridiculous. "Maybe I'd pick a princess name for myself. Aurora? Belle?"

"What's your plan?" he asked softly. "What are you going to do to slip that weight?"

"Like Josh said in the car. I have my own secrets. You have yours."

"Maybe secrets aren't doing anyone any favors. Maybe we could help each other."

"Maybe," I said. "You tell me yours first."

He hesitated, chewing on his toothpick.

"That's what I thought," I said.

He took it out of his mouth and tucked it into the pocket on his flannel shirt. "I guess we have to get to know each other better."

"You sure you wouldn't rather get to know Misty?" My voice gave away a bit too much of my insecurity, and I bit down on my lower lip.

He smiled slightly. "I don't know. Should I?"

"No." There was a raw edge in my voice. I didn't know it was going to be there, or I would have swallowed the word.

"No. She's a nice girl, and she seems perfect but…I don't think a nice girl is what I'm looking for." His voice was low.

We were so close that his eyes were a warm blur as he looked into mine. His lips were softly parted, inviting and kissable.

"I hope I get to know you," he said.

"Maybe," I said.

He closed the faint distance between us, his lips grazing mine. It was just the faintest, briefest nuzzle, and then he was gone, leaning away. His eyes were intent, gauging my reaction.

That faint, tentative kiss left my lips throbbing, as if I had to kiss him again.

But he was already climbing to his feet. He held out his hand, offering me help up.

"Come on, Piper," he said. "Back to reality."

"Reality, where we're both late," I said. I took his hand, just for a second to let him help me up, even though I didn't need it. His hands were warm and firm, and my thumb slid across calloused knuckles as he lifted me easily.

"I think we're in a lot more trouble than just being late," he said, but he said it lightly, as if trouble didn't scare him.

As we walked toward the now-likely-locked doors back to school, I wasn't scared of trouble either. The fear would be back soon. It always was.

But for now, there wasn't room for fear when I had this strange flutter in my chest.

11

That afternoon, I walked out of the front doors of the school and toward the parking lot. I stopped by Josh's car, but the guys were nowhere to be seen.

Misty almost walked past me, heading for the last row, and then she stopped and turned around. She tossed her long, silky brown hair over her shoulder. "Waiting for Josh?"

"He gave me a ride to school," I said it casually, but I didn't mean it casually. Oh my god. I glanced toward school. If Kai heard that, he'd totally take back the *you don't seem like a kid* compliment. I was being so high school.

She nodded. "Well, sorry. But he and Kai are meeting with the football coach."

"Football?" I asked.

"Apparently, they were both really good in their hometown," she said, tucking a long strand of hair behind her ear. Her eyes lingered on my cheek. Her tone was different, softer, when she asked, "How's it going for you lately, Piper?"

"Fine," I said woodenly.

She nodded. She seemed like she wanted to say something else, but she just smiled at me. "All right. Do you want a ride home?"

"I've got to get Maddie," I said. "I'll walk. But thanks."

Just then, the Mustang turned into the parking lot. My heart froze in my chest. But Callum's face was inside, his broad shoulders filling the front seat. I drew a deep breath, filling my lungs before I realized I'd stopped breathing when I saw the Mustang.

Misty stared at me as if she could read my expressions. Then, as if she'd remembered we had to pretend there was nothing wrong in my life, she asked, "Are you coming to Spirit Night? We haven't hung out in ages!"

"No," I said. I would love to spend more time with Josh and Kai. I was not going to punish myself by watching Josh flirt with Misty if I had a choice. Hard pass. "Have fun!"

I opened the passenger door and slid into the soft leather seat.

"Hey kiddo, how was school?" Callum said. He put the car into drive as I rushed to close the door.

His voice was warm and teasing, but suddenly my mood was even lower than it had been seeing Misty. He saw me as a kid, when I had a definite crush on him. *Kiddo*. There was something so familiar and sweet in that word, but it was just a joke to him. And of course, my own dad was never picking me up from school and asking me those questions.

"Piper?" he asked, a note of uncertainty in his low, sexy voice.

"It was great," I said. "Did you have the day off?"

He nodded. "I'm still getting into the swing of things."

"You work at the big hospital in the city?" Blissford wasn't big enough for our own hospital, although we did have an urgent care center I'd visited a time or ten.

"Yeah. Were you born there?"

I grinned. "You and your nephews have the weirdest questions. You guys making a documentary about Blissford?"

"Just curious," he said. "I hope you haven't had anything more serious to go to the hospital for."

When he said that, his gaze lingered on my face before he turned his attention back to the road.

I rubbed my fingertips across the bruises absently. And then I winced. *Yeah, they still hurt.*

"Drive over to the elementary school, okay?" I asked. "I've got to pick up my little sister."

"You have a sister?"

"Yeah. Maddie. She's nine."

He nodded. The elementary school was only a few blocks away, and when we arrived, he swiveled to get out of the driver's side.

Maddie waited on the sidewalk, and I hugged her hello, crushing her hot pink puffy jacket into my side. She looped her arms around my neck and squeezed back. Usually, she was too cool for me when we were in front of her friends now, but sometimes she seemed to read I'd had a bad day.

Then her eyes fixed past me, on Callum standing on the sidewalk. "Who's that?"

"A friend," I said quickly. A friend we were never ever going to mention to Dad.

Callum held out the keys. The front bumper of the car was all shiny, untouched silver; it looked as though I'd never fishtailed across a highway.

"Thank you," I said gratefully, taking the keys.

"Take care of yourself." He nodded goodbye and turned, heading in the direction of the high school.

"Wait," I said. "Do you want a ride home? You don't need to wait for Josh and Kai. I can take you back."

"Are you sure?" he asked.

I nodded. "It's the least I can do."

"You don't owe me anything, Piper," he said firmly. "He should never have been out running like that."

It took me a second to connect *he* with the white dog from the night before.

"Is he a new dog?" I asked. "Kai said he didn't have a name yet."

"Very new," he said. "Quite the handful."

I nodded. "Well, I don't mind driving you home, anyway."

"Then thank you," he said. "If you're sure it won't be any trouble."

He leaned forward, holding his hand out to shake Maddie's hand. "Hi. I'm Callum."

"Maddie. Are you a friend of my sister's?"

"We just met each other," he said. "But I hope so."

"Good," Maddie said. "She really needs some friends."

"Brutal honesty from the nine-year-old," I muttered, opening the back door for her. "Get in, Mads. Stop embarrassing me."

"It's just beginning," she said, sliding into the backseat obediently with her overstuffed backpack.

"Maddie," I warned. She grinned in response, which wasn't a good sign. Maddie had all the lightness and mischief you'd expect from a youngest child. I'd done my best to shelter her.

And this was the thanks I got: frank conversations about my lacking social life with my inappropriate crush.

By the time I swung into the driver's seat, Callum was in the passenger seat, and he was saying, "I'd expect Piper to have a lot of friends. She seems like a great girl."

"She is," Maddie said. "She used to be one of the popular kids."

"That's a stretch," I muttered. I started to pull away from the curb, but I had to stop to adjust the seat forward. Callum had long legs to go with those big shoulders.

"You drive like a grandma," Callum said. "Right up against the steering wheel."

Maddie laughed, a surprising loud peal of laughter, and I pulled a face. "The two of you are ganging up on me? That seems unfair."

"So what happened?" Callum asked.

I ignored the question. "Were you popular in high school? You seem like you would have been popular."

"I was a teenage foster kid," he said frankly. "I ended up going to five different high schools, and I don't think I was popular at any of them."

"You seem to have bad luck in your family," I said, and then bit my lip, realizing how inappropriate that was to blurt out. Good grief. I'd just been so surprised he'd been in foster care when Josh and Kai and Nick had all also lost their parents.

"Yeah," he said, with faint bitterness in his words. "It feels like a curse."

"But your luck has changed, right?" I said lightly. He was a doctor now, after all. He had to have been pretty successful in the past several years.

"We'll see."

It was such a mysterious way to put it. To Maddie, I said, "My new *friends* are full of mysteries."

"Friends?" she asked casually.

Callum turned toward the window, but not fast enough for me to miss his sudden smile. "You aren't as good at keeping secrets as I thought, Piper."

"Callum has three *nephews*," I said. "He's pretty old, huh?"

That earned me his gaze back, and a distinctly dour look.

"I'm not that old," he said, his voice low and warm and sexy. A completely inappropriate rush of warmth flooded my body.

Maddie leaned forward, staring at Callum's face in profile as if she was scrutinizing him. Callum ducked his head, no longer able to hide his smile.

"Do I pass your inspection?" he asked her teasingly.

"You don't look that old," she pronounced.

"Thank you."

"And for old as you are, you actually look pretty cute. Like a movie star."

"Maddie!" I said, scandalized. "You're nine! You can't notice if guys are cute. Good grief."

"Like I'm going to watch a movie and not realize Alex Pettyfer or Zac Effron is why you picked it out? Please." She shook her head. "Speaking of. Dad's poker night is Saturday—what are we watching?"

"Something animated," I said.

"You can't stop me from growing up," Maddie said.

Callum grinned.

I side-eyed him as we took the turn onto the long country road that led to their strange estate. "Don't encourage her."

He raised his hands innocently. "You can tell you're sisters."

"What does that mean?" Maddie asked. I was glad she asked, because I definitely wanted to know what he meant.

"You're both quite sharp."

"Do you like smart girls?" Maddie asked.

Callum's grin widened. "I'm not dating. But, if I were, I would definitely prefer a smart woman."

Well, this was fun. Discussing my hopeless crush's interests in *women* with my little sister. But still, I felt light and silly with the two of them. It was a nice change from being so worried all the time.

"Piper is days from being a woman," Maddie said.

"That's enough of that," I said quickly, my cheeks blazing.

"Well, technically, you aren't a girl once you're eighteen," she said.

"Where do you get this stuff?" I demanded.

Callum stifled a laugh at my discomfort as I took the turn for his driveway. Maddie's eyes widened as we bounced over the long trail down to the house. "It's like a castle!" she said. "Hidden in the woods!"

"Well, you're both welcome here anytime," Callum said. "Since you're a pair of princesses."

I wasn't sure how to take that, but he was already throwing open his door. I hurried to brake, although he stepped lightly out of the car while it was still rolling to a stop.

He turned back, his hand on the top of the door, and leaned inside. "I do mean that, Piper. You always have somewhere to come."

I nodded, a sudden lump in my throat.

He hesitated. Glancing into the backseat, he smiled at Maddie. "It was nice meeting you."

Maddie said goodbye to him, then his eyes flickered to me. He hesitated, as if he wanted to say something more, before he nodded. He shut the door firmly behind him and headed for the house.

Just for a second, I watched him go. His fitted jacket clung to his broad shoulders, but the most magnetic thing about him was the swagger in his walk.

He turned back at the porch steps, looking back at our car, which hadn't moved yet, and raised his hand in a goodbye. I hurried to put the car into drive, before turning around and pulling back out down his driveway.

Maddie raised her hand to cover her mouth, bending over at the waist like she was going to pass out from suppressed amusement.

"Don't even," I said.

"What?" she asked, straightening. "I like making new friends. Getting to know people. Just like you."

I pulled a face, and she burst out laughing. I smiled at her in the rearview mirror. Maddie might have been my little sister—and the one I had to protect—but in some ways, she was the best friend I had. We always had each other, even when it seemed like the world was against us.

I wouldn't risk my chance to protect her for any crush.

All the lightness I felt around the guys fell away as we pulled in the driveway of our own house. Dad wasn't home yet. I couldn't help the sense of an impending storm as Maddie and I got snacks and sat down to do our homework at the kitchen island. At four-thirty, I put a frozen lasagna in the oven and made a salad, making sure dinner would be ready. Then I did a loop through the house, putting away wayward shoes and books and Barbie dolls. I wanted to make sure there was no reason for Dad to be mad.

Well, no reason besides having to look at my face, after what had happened the night before.

When I returned to the kitchen island, Maddie was picking at her lower lip, which she sometimes did until it bled. I pushed her hand away from her mouth. "Go use your Chapstick."

Dad hated it when her lips were raw and bleeding. Her anxiety was one of the little bits of evidence that anyone could have used to tell there was something wrong, if they cared.

The garage door rumbled open. Maddie's eyes met mine, widening, but I tried to smile. "Go on. I'll call you when it's dinner time."

She shoved her homework folder into her backpack and threw her backpack into the organizer by the garage door, then ran upstairs. The island was already clean, but I sprayed it and started wiping it with a paper towel, just to look productive when he came in.

The door opened, and my father dropped his bag on the bench between the garage and the kitchen. He didn't even look at me. "Did you bring Maddie home from school?"

"She's upstairs. Dinner should be ready in twenty minutes or so."

"Good." He walked through the kitchen toward the living room, his eyes still on everything but me. His salt-and-pepper hair was brushed back from his face. "Before we eat, go put your stuff away. It's scattered all over the place."

I nodded. That was as close as he was going to come to acknowledging what had happened yesterday and saying that I could have my stuff back.

"Call me when dinner is ready," he said. "I'm going to eat in my study. I've got a lot to do tonight."

"I will," I said. As soon as the door to his study clicked shut, I ran to the garage to move my things.

It was strange to walk back into that cement space and throw a garbage bag of stuffed animals over my shoulder, then bend to pick up the laundry basket full of my clothes. In front of me were the metal shelves I'd thrown my father into...somehow. I still didn't know where the strength had come from. The cars were parked neatly under the fluorescent lights, everything tidy, the way our lives were supposed to look.

When I had carried everything upstairs, I was glad to bring out the last load of my things and close the door behind me. I still carried the bruises from that night, and I would for a while.

But not forever.

12

Nick

"It still sounds quiet," Josh said. His head was cocked to one side, listening intently.

"She's all right," I said, but I didn't want to leave her. It had been hours since her father came home, and nothing had happened.

Piper's blinds were open, and her room was brightly lit. The back windows of the house looked out toward the woods, and she probably didn't imagine anyone would be lurking in the woods, watching after her.

From here, we'd watched her as she shook her comforter over her bed and climbed on top of it, straightening the corners. We watched her put books and stuffed animals in her bookshelves. All the while, we waited in case things turned south.

Now, she pulled her shirt over her head, a sudden motion that made my breath catch in my chest. I hadn't expected to see her undress. A black bra cupped her pale breasts above a narrow waist.

She pulled her blonde hair back with her hands, smoothing it, and then twisting it into a bun.

Josh smacked me in the chest. "Come on. Give her some privacy." His voice was gruff.

"Sorry." I turned my back on her, with effort. I could still remember the shape of her body, her beautiful face under the bruises, and I wouldn't forget it. It wasn't just her beauty that drew me to her, though. Quiet strength shone out of her sad eyes, and in the sudden smile that brightened her face like sunshine on a cold winter's day.

There was the faintest ruffle from the forest, and Josh and I exchanged a look. I took a step forward, ready for a fight, even though my leg still felt weak.

"What the hell are you two doing?" Callum stepped out of the brush, still pulling on his t-shirt from the change. He tweaked the hem so it fell over his abs.

"Nothing," Josh said. "Just looking after her. Just in case."

"Just." Callum shook his head, but then he glanced toward the house. He quickly averted his eyes, staring down at the ground for a second before his gaze flickered to us instead. "Well? Is she fine?"

We nodded.

"But you were hanging around..." He gestured toward the house.

"It's not like that," I said.

"You're already on thin ice," Callum said, his jaw tightening. "You're lucky you didn't change back when you got hit. Given all that adrenaline, and your total lack of control—"

"I know," I said. "I'm sorry."

"But we couldn't leave her here alone, in case..." Josh shrugged, instead of filling in the horrible things we thought might happen to her.

"What would you do?" Callum asked. "Would you run in there as boys or as wolves?"

"Neither of us are boys." Josh's eyes met his in challenge.

Callum stared at him, not backing down. "Do you have something you want to say, Josh? Something you want to do?"

Josh finally looked away, his jaw tight. He shook his head.

"Good," Callum said. Now that Josh had submitted, he folded his arms over his chest, his expression softening. "I don't blame you for looking after the girl. Even if your plan is half-assed."

"She's special," Josh said. "Are you sure she isn't...?"

Callum shook his head. "Misty is the one with the questionable hospital records. I know it would be nice to think you could take Piper away from here, away from that monster...but he really is her father."

"I just don't feel it," Josh muttered. "With Misty."

"It could take time," Callum said. "And anyway, when she was hidden, they would have dulled her powers. It might be why she can't feel you any more than you can feel her."

"Or it might not be here," I said, giving voice to the fear we all shared. "It might be another false lead."

"I'm pretty sure," Callum said. "Someone forged her birth records. And we won't be able to break it until we get closer, but someone enchanted her."

"Our cover story sucks, by the way," Josh said, but there was humor in his voice. Callum wouldn't take it personally. "Your nephews?"

"Lord knows it feels like you're my kids." Callum cuffed him in the back of the head, playfully. "You're all pains in the ass."

"Must be nice to be too old to go back to high school," Kai said from the shadows. He stepped into the faint circle of light cast by the moonlight in this space within the trees where we had gathered. He wore boots, visible under the hem of his jeans, and a leather jacket, so he must have walked here unchanged.

"Yup," Callum admitted. "Sorry, I'm not sorry. You three can suffer. Right now, I have to say you deserve high school."

"Yeah?" Kai asked. "Did you leave the house to follow them or to check on Piper?"

"A little of column A, a little of column B." Callum crossed his arms. "Don't you have homework to do?"

Josh groaned. "Well, do football players at Blissford High really do their homework? I'm doubting it."

"I'm glad you impressed the coach." Callum's tone suggested we hadn't managed to impress him. "Now let's give it every chance you have to win over Misty, hm? She has a good thing in Blissford. You have to make a good impression for her to give the pack a chance."

"If she is the one." Josh said rebelliously.

"If she is the one," Callum conceded. "And anyway, Piper mentioned her father will be playing poker on game night. She should be safe here."

"She mentioned that?" Kai asked, false-innocent, thrusting his hands into his jacket pockets. He was chewing on a toothpick again, absently. It must be a habit he'd picked up when the pack was torn apart. We'd spent so many years away from each other. All of us had our bad habits and damage from that time.

I hadn't remembered any of them, honestly, when Callum walked into my life and changed everything. I'd been a baby when the pack was destroyed.

"Yeah," Callum said.

Kai leaned against a tree, his hands tucked into his pockets. "When did you get the chance to chat?"

"When you boys were sweet-talking the coach," Callum said coolly. "I brought Piper her father's Mustang."

"You're the hero of the day for sure," Kai said.

Callum's voice went dangerously soft. "Stay on track, Kai. We won't have a whole pack until we find our girl."

"I'm on track," Kai promised.

Callum nodded, but he didn't look pacified. "See you back at the house."

He pulled his shirt over his head as he walked back into the dark forest, his bare feet almost silent. As he lifted the shirt, his muscles rippled beneath the jagged scars and tattoos on his back, a web of ink and damage.

He'd gone through a lot to save us all, and then to bring us back together. I glanced toward Kai, wondering if he thought about the same things.

Kai's toothpick bobbed on his lip, his face as inscrutable as ever. "I've got to human it back. Anyone want to walk with me?"

"Yeah, we will," Josh said. He glanced one more time back at the house. In the window, we could see Piper, still silhouetted, reading a book. Her face was sweet in profile: an upturned nose, petal-soft pink lips pressed together. She twined her hair absently between her fingers as she read.

Kai stared at her, too. Something like raw longing crossed his face, then he must have felt my gaze, because he glared at me. Anger chased away every other emotion.

"She's nothing," Kai said roughly. "You heard Callum. There's no chance she's the pack princess. Move on, Nick."

"I am," I said.

Kai shook his head, as if he was angry, and stalked off into the woods.

"Great company to walk with," I said. I followed him, but Josh still stood, watching her.

"Come on," I said. "She's fine for tonight."

He hesitated, then nodded, falling in beside me.

"I feel like we're missing something," he said.

The walk hurt my leg, but I deserved every twinge that radiated up my shin through my thigh. I winced. "It's not that complicated, Josh. We went through hell, we see someone sweet like her suffering, we want to help. It doesn't mean she's special. It just means she feels more like us than Misty does."

Misty was cute and bubbly and sweet, but there didn't seem to be depth there, the kind of potential for understanding each other I felt with Piper.

Not that Piper felt any of that bond. Most of the time we'd spent together, I'd been a wolf.

"Funny how you don't say much," Josh said, "but when you do say something, you've got it all figured out."

"I don't know about that," I said.

If I had things all figured out, I wouldn't be pining for a girl who couldn't be mine.

My heart belonged to a girl born almost eighteen years ago, our blessing—and the harbinger of our curse.

13

P*iper*

WATCHING Josh flirt with Misty was a special kind of hell.

He bumped his shoulder into hers as they walked into class, and she turned her face up to him, glancing up at him through her eyelashes. He grinned his easy, confident smile, his teeth white above that square jaw. He really was movie-star pretty, just like Callum. My little sister wasn't wrong.

"Did you write me a song yet?" she teased, bumping her shoulder back into his.

"That's Nick's department," he told her. "He writes lyrics. I mostly focus on melodies."

"I still can't picture you playing the guitar," she said.

"I'm pretty good." He put his arm around her waist and ran his fingers rapidly over her side, as if she were a guitar whose strings he was plucking. She giggled as she captured his hand, pressing his fingers flat against her stomach. "You'll see one day."

"Football game on Friday night and the tease of a concert one day? Who are you trying to impress?" she teased.

"I doubt I'll get any playing time Friday," he said. "Or ever. I'm the new guy—Coach was good to get me in."

"You didn't answer my question," she said.

"You," he said simply. She laughed and slipped out of his grip, sliding into the chair in front of me. Glossy brown hair whipped across my desktop, yet again.

Josh's eyes met mine. For once, that grin of his dropped away. The look he gave me was bleak, almost helpless. Deep blue eyes gazed into mine.

I glanced away, looking toward the door, as the teacher walked in. I could not. For some reason, my chest grew tight when I looked at Josh's stupid face, like I was going to cry.

Josh sat down and then, after a second, leaned over my shoulder. "Are you going to come to the game?"

I shook my head, not bothering to look back.

"Football's not your thing?" His tone was false-light. "You and Misty could come together."

Yeah, that sounded like a party for sure.

"My dad won't let me," I said. "Pretty sure I'm grounded."

And grateful for it, for once.

He shifted in his seat. I could have sworn I felt the heat from his body, even though he couldn't be that close with his elbows on the desk behind me, as he leaned over to whisper into my ear. "I've got practice after school."

"Good for you."

"I didn't mean—" he broke off, impatiently.

I twisted in my seat, finally. "I mean it. Good for you. That's what you wanted, right?"

He sighed. It didn't sound as if he was crazy about football.

I wasn't crazy about this conversation. I twisted in my seat, but even as the teacher began taking attendance, Josh leaned forward, as if he had something more to say. I ignored him as pointedly as I could. I was not talking to Josh.

I had good reason not to be talking to Josh; it was rude to talk in homeroom while the teacher was speaking. It had nothing to do with my ridiculous feelings being hurt.

Josh whispered in my ear, trying to draw me into conversation, but I wasn't having it.

When we left class, he and Misty were talking about Trig, and the two of them walked ahead of me. I drifted toward my first class of the day.

Then, all of a sudden, Josh grabbed my forearm and pushed me down a side hall, out of the stream of bodies. I glanced down the empty hall; the unoccupied auditorium was the only thing down here.

"What do you want?" I hissed.

He glanced back, checking if there was anyone to see us—there wasn't—and then pulled me behind him through a door. Suddenly we were in the dimly lit space behind the stage. Thick red curtains hung around us.

I pulled my arm out of his grip, although I had to admit to a kind of dangerous curiosity.

"Sorry," he said.

"Sorry for what?" I demanded.

His big hands cupped my cheeks. I stared up at him, perplexed.

"For acting like I don't want to do this," he said, and then pressed his lips against mine.

Josh's lips were soft and warm. His lower lip lingered against mine, his deep blue eyes steady, gauging my reaction.

I didn't pull away. Instead, I stared back at him. "Why did you kiss me?"

"You looked sad."

"I don't need pity kisses."

"And I wanted to." His forehead met mine, his eyelashes drifting shut. He held my face against his. "I wanted to so badly. Is that wrong?"

"I guess I don't mind it," I said, which was the understatement of the year.

His grip on my face loosened. Before he could let go, I pressed my lips against his.

He tasted like black coffee and peppermint Chapstick, and my lips tingled when we traded kisses. He kissed my lower lip, thoughtfully, as if kissing away the pout he'd put there.

I guessed I hadn't done a very good job hiding my feelings when Josh and Misty were playing around.

I wrapped my hands around his wrists. "Are you going to kiss Misty too?"

His eyes clouded. "Piper."

"What?" I asked. "If you're making a bid for popularity—if you're going to win that bet—you might as well date the most popular girl in the school."

"You have to wonder why everyone finds her so charming," he muttered. "If she's really blessed with something special…"

Well, those words were a stab into my chest. I gazed up at him, trying to push away the roil of emotions I couldn't even make sense of. Was I angry or sad or jealous or just a fool, crazy to kiss him again?

All of the above?

"I don't want to talk about her," he said, his eyes fixed on mine. "I'm not supposed to be doing this."

I raised my eyebrows. "I definitely am not allowed to date. But Callum doesn't seem like he would rein you in like that."

His lips twisted. "I don't want to talk about Callum either, right now."

I put my palms on his rock-hard chest and pushed him away, gently. "Well, there's no reason not to."

"It's kind of a mood-killer."

"Your crush on Misty was already killing my mood." I crinkled my nose at him. "What, you think you're going to date her and have me on the side? What do you think I am?"

"I think you're great," he said. "I'm not—that's not what I want. I don't have a crush on Misty."

I crossed my arms over my chest, leveling him a look.

"I can't explain right now," he said. "But I will eventually. Can you just trust me?"

I shook my head. No, no I couldn't.

"That's fair, I guess," he muttered, but he swiped his hand through his hair. "Come on, Piper."

"I don't know what you want from me." My lips still tingled from the kisses we'd traded. I took a step back, almost falling into the curtain behind me, but I caught myself, gripping fistfuls of red velvet.

"I've never felt this way about anyone else," he said softly. "Look at me."

Reluctantly, I met his deep blue eyes. He closed the distance between us again, his hands wrapping around my hips possessively. His gaze was tortured, full of affection at the same time as he bit down on his lower lip, as if he was holding himself back.

"There's one girl I want," he said, his voice rough. "And she's the only one I look at this way. No matter how else I can *act*, I can't fake this."

His words—and his gaze—and his lips hovering so near mine left my core throbbing, a warm glow spiking through my chest. This man devastated me in the best of ways.

"Forget you," I said fiercely. My very desire for him left me angry. "You can't talk to me like this, look at me like this, while you're—"

"We both have our secrets," he interrupted me, his voice low and hungry.

I gripped his powerful biceps in my hands, but I couldn't quite bring myself to shove him away.

Those eyes seemed to stare right into my soul.

Unable to resist him, I suddenly bobbed up onto my toes, still gripping his arms for balance, and kissed him hard. I pressed my lips to the side of his kissable mouth, and he turned his head, trying to catch my lips again.

"When you figure out what you want," I whispered, my lips grazing his cheek, "come tell me."

I meant to push him away, but somehow when I tried, he drew me with him, pulling my body against his. His fingers tangled in my hair, tugging my scalp, as he turned my face to his. He kissed me again, wildly, hungrily, and despite myself, I kissed him back. The two of us stumbled in the curtains, red wrapping around us, gripping each other tightly.

I finally pulled away, my chest heaving, trying to catch my breath after the kisses we'd traded. He wrapped his arms around me, and I leaned against the warm solidity of his chest.

"You're crazy," I said softly, "and you're going to make me crazy too."

He smiled, just enough to turn up the edges of his firm mouth. I took his jaw in my hand, unable to resist touching the angles of his cheekbones.

"It's your fault," he said. "Look at that face of yours." He stroked my cheek with the back of a finger, the touch of his calloused knuckle rough and tender all at once. "All that kindness and strength and sweetness wrapped up in one beautiful package. I can't help it, Piper."

The way he looked at me, and the things he said, were overwhelming. No one thought as much of me as he seemed to, and it made me foolish.

I pulled the curtain between us, hiding from his handsome face. I needed time to catch my breath. He laughed, his hands reaching through the velvet to catch me.

"We're going to be late," I said. My voice came out low with desire, as full of confusion as I felt.

"We're worse than late," he said, and his hands closed on my hips, even through the velvet. I could see the shape of his broad shoulders and his head, outlined through the fabric. "Might as well skip class now."

"You've got to go to your classes, though." I ducked under the hem of the curtain, the heavy fabric brushing across my hair, and straightened in the fresh, cool air. My chest was still heaving with the effort and with my wayward emotions, no matter how cool I tried to sound. "You have practice this afternoon."

He groaned. He stepped back out of the curtains himself, running a hand through his mussed blond hair. "Piper."

"Josh." I popped my hands on my hips. "I meant what I said. When you figure out what you're doing, you know where to find me."

"I know what I want," he said.

"That's not what I said." I headed for the door. "I said when you know what you're *doing*."

"Piper," he said, his voice low and full of frustration.

I closed the door on him anyway, leaving him behind me.

14

"I've been thinking," Maddie said. Her nose was red, her hood pulled up over her curly blond hair.

"Uh-oh," I said. We were almost to school, and I couldn't stop looking around for Eli, expecting him to pop up at any moment. I couldn't come up with a more clever response. Luckily, Maddie didn't seem to notice how distracted I was.

"We should go somewhere fun!" she said. "We have *never* been on vacation. Not ever."

I couldn't imagine us and Dad riding the teacups at Disneyland together, but I didn't want to say that. She was only nine years old, after all.

"Yeah?" I said. "Where do you want to go?"

I expected her to say Disney—it was the morning of my eighteenth birthday and I was still sad I'd never had the chance to go—but instead she said, "I was thinking Europe!"

I hid a grin. "Europe, huh? What do you know about Europe?"

She flashed me her most scornful look. "What do *you* know about Europe? There's London. There's the cliffs of Dover. There's France. Paris is where Sabrina turned into a woman."

We'd watched *Sabrina* a few months before, during one of our girls' movie nights. Apparently, Audrey Hepburn had left quite the impression on my little sister.

In case I'd missed the implication, she added, "You should really go to Paris."

"I'll put it on my bucket list," I said, "but I don't think we're going anywhere anytime soon."

She sighed heavily. "Well, I think an eighteenth birthday deserves a big celebration."

I patted the top of her hood. "All I want is cupcakes with my best girl."

Actually, all I wanted was custody of Maddie and my own place, but I couldn't tell her any of that.

"You need friends your age," Maddie said.

It was my turn to sigh heavily. "Well, I'll see you after school."

"You'll be right here?" Despite the way she usually spoke—so grown-up in such a petite blond package—she looked up at me with anxious gray-blue eyes. She had a fear of being left behind, for some reason. Maybe it was because she'd never had the chance to know our mom. She rarely gave it away anymore—she was learning how to hide her feelings, like all kids have to—but that fear must still have lingered under the surface.

"Aren't I always?" I said. "I'm always right here. Because I don't have any friends."

As much as I meant to reassure her, I couldn't help teasing too. She rolled her eyes—well, that was a new and annoying skill—and threw a wave over her shoulder as she turned and headed into school.

I watched her go, her pink backpack bouncing on her thin shoulders. She seemed so little and so grown-up at the same time. I couldn't imagine leaving without her. I couldn't imagine going to sleep in another city, alone and safe, not knowing if she was sleeping safely in her bed or if our father was going to hurt her too. Maybe without me around, he'd turn on her as viciously as he'd done with me.

My plan had to work.

"Piper!" Eli's voice sounded sharp as a whip and way too close to me, right over my shoulder. I stiffened just before he threw his arm over my shoulders. The intense scent of his body spray enveloped me.

"Hi, Eli," I said flatly.

"Tonight," he said, "the football game, then the after-party. Sound like a plan?"

"For our date?" That word, *date*, burned in my mouth, "You want me to watch you play football?"

"Your dad never lets you out of the house otherwise, huh?" he asked. "Unless you're with me?"

I wouldn't be face-to-face with Eli during the game. I couldn't do much better for a date with him. And Josh and Kai, and probably Nick in the audience, would be there. Excitement spiked through my chest.

"I don't think he'll let me go to the party," I said. "But yeah, I'll go to the game."

Eli shot me a skeptical look, as if surprised I'd agreed so quickly. "He won't know about the party. We'll go for an hour. Two, tops."

"Eli," I said. "You're going to get me in trouble."

"You've got to live a little," he said.

"I'm trying," I muttered.

"I've got to be at the game an hour early. Do you mind?" he asked.

Oh my god, after everything he'd done to me earlier, now he was talking like this was a real date. Like we were starting all over.

"No, I don't mind," I managed.

"I'll pick you up at your house at five," he said.

"I'll have to ask my dad," I said. "I don't know for sure he'll say yes."

"He'll say yes," Eli said confidently. Maybe he had every reason to be confident. After all, I was pretty sure he was a teenaged version of my father. The two of them should like each other.

"As long as he says yes, I'll be ready at five," I said.

He squeezed my shoulders. "Good girl."

Funny how those words made me feel like anything but a good girl. They made me feel dirty.

If my plan worked, though, I'd leave Eli behind me soon.

I'd also be leaving Josh and Kai and Nick. For some reason, that made me feel sad, but I barely knew them. I shouldn't care about that.

Still, I couldn't help but look toward the student parking lot as Eli and I headed into school, still linked together. He wouldn't let go of his vice-like grip on my shoulders.

Josh got out of the driver's seat of his car. Kai said something to him over the top of the car, and Josh laughed, throwing back his head. Kai ducked his head, a faint satisfied smile across his lips. God, they were both so gorgeous. Nick climbed out of the backseat, gripping the car door hard, like he was hurt. I frowned.

"What're you looking at?" Eli squeezed my shoulders, hard. He must have followed my gaze.

"Nothing," I nodded toward Nick. "New guy."

Josh stared at me and Eli. The expression on his face froze, as if he wore a mask. The smile was gone.

Kai said something, and Nick turned toward us as he shut his door. Three pairs of eyes stared at us—brown, blue, green—as cold and unfriendly as the day I'd met them. It felt unsettling when they'd been so warm the last time I talked to them.

"Yeah," he said. "The other two guys just joined the team."

"Are they any good?"

"Not that good," he said, a sour note in his voice.

I'd planned to break away from Eli, but I couldn't now. If I tried to leave him, he'd think I was headed toward Josh. He would never let me get away.

But right now, I needed to slip all of them.

Today would be the day I saved myself.

I SLIPPED out of school after homeroom, keenly aware of just how much of a tight timeline I was on. I ran home and grabbed my tapes from the Nanny-cam bear. I wished I had some way to convert the old tapes to digital files, something I could email to myself. I hated that I had no way to back them up. But, the bear was the best I could do. I pulled my books out and stacked them on the desk, shoving the bear and the tapes in my backpack instead. Then I rifled through everything, taking every bit of cash I still had together in my wallet.

When I walked up the wide stone steps to the police station in town, I felt like everyone was watching me, like my father would be called before I could even talk to a police officer, like he was going to come sweep me out of there before I had the chance to do anything.

But by lunch time, I was in a judge's office, with the town sheriff standing by the door. He crossed his arms, shaking his head, as the tapes played on the old TV they'd found.

They were hard for me to watch, and I'd already lived through them. My father snarled into my face, shoved me against the wall, hit me with his belt over and over. I glanced away from the video footage, feeling my stomach tight and sick, as if he'd hurt me all over again.

"I'm sorry that happened to you," the sheriff said. "Your father took it too far."

I glanced toward the judge, who was quiet but looked sympathetic enough. "I'm really just worried about my sister now. Can I get custody of her? Because I'm eighteen now, and what if he hurts her too—"

"Oh, honey," the judge said. "Your father is never going to do that to her. Or to you, ever again."

"Good," I said. Relief spread through my chest, and for the first time I realized just how much of a burden I usually did carry.

"Do you have copies of the tapes?" the sheriff asked.

"No," I said.

"We're going to take these into evidence," he said, ejecting the tape from the TV. "That way we have them when we need them."

"Okay," I said. "So what happens for the protection order?"

"Honey," the judge said, "what we're going to do is a little different today."

The sheriff took the tapes and the bear and stepped out of the room. The door clicked shut behind him.

Anxiety wrapped so tight around my chest that I could barely breathe.

"What's that?" I asked, my voice flat.

"I'm going to talk to your father and make sure he never hurts you again," the judge said. "Don't worry. I won't tell him about any of this."

I stared at him. I couldn't even form words. How in the world was he going to 'talk' to my father without making it obvious I'd gone looking for help? And why should I trust him, anyway?

"Are you going to be at my dad's poker night Saturday?" My voice sounded distant, far-away.

"Piper," he said kindly. He leaned forward, folding his hands together, his elbows braced against his knees. "It's obvious you've been thinking about this plan for a long time. You put together the best plan you could, didn't you—a girl alone in the world, trying to study up on the solution to all your problems?"

That was jarringly accurate. I shook my head anyway, although the part of me that could see myself at a distance didn't know why I was shaking my head. It was true. I'd spent all those furtive afternoons, searching law online, clearing out the cache on my web searches so my father wouldn't run across them, learning different ways to steal and hide a little money for a chance at a new life.

"You did the best you could alone," he said. "But it was never going to work."

His voice was gentle, and that made it worse. Hot tears stung my eyes, and I looked up at the ceiling, blinking them back.

"No one is going to give you custody of Maddie," he said. "You don't have a job. You don't have a place to live. She's not better off with you when you'll be homeless."

"I won't be for long," I said. "I'll figure it out."

"No one's going to believe you," he said.

"I have the tapes." My voice came out hot.

"That was a good try," he said. "But do you know how many

people would agree with your father that it was just discipline?"

I rubbed my finger across the bruises, still vivid against my cheek and jaw. They ached under my touch, but I pressed harder, reminding myself that what happened was real. There was no video of this beating. But who could watch the video and deny it happened? Who could say my father was right?

"We don't live in a society where children have many rights," he said. "You're not going to get what you want from this...I'm trying to help you."

"I told you what I need," I said.

"I'll talk to your father," he said. "I'll say the bruises came to my attention. No one will know we had this meeting, Piper."

"And then what?" I asked dully. "How does Maddie get out of there?"

"She grows up," he said. "Just like you'll do. And you'll move on with your lives."

"So that's it? We just have to survive? Nine more years." I leaned forward, my voice growing louder with every word.

"That's it," he said. "If you try to push it—if you go to another police station in another county—your father will find out. And you and your sister will still be in his custody, in his house. Maybe Child Protective Services watching will make your father more cautious, for a while."

I was going to be sick. I turned away, staring over his shoulder out the window. Outside, red and gold leaves danced in the breeze. It was a beautiful, sunny fall day.

"It was a good try," he said. "Sometimes you lose the battle. You have to focus on winning the war."

He was one of my father's friends, I was sure of it.

That didn't mean he was wrong.

I stood up. "Thank you for your time."

"I'm sorry I don't have better news," he said. "Be careful out there, Piper."

"I always am," I said.

Thanks to people like him, I had to be.

15

I texted my father, asking for permission to go out with Eli, and he texted back *Yes*.

I sighed as I turned my cell phone in my hands.

"Done," Maddie said, sliding her math homework into her folder. "What movie are we watching tonight?"

We'd been working our way through a list of the top one hundred classic romance movies, which, come to think of it, might have been breaking my sister's young brain.

"We're not," I said. "I've got a date."

"With Callum?" she asked, cocking her head to one side.

"No," I said. I wish. I could just imagine tucking my arm into his big, muscular arm, feeling safe and protected as the two of us walked through town. No, wait, I *didn't* wish—he was too old for me.

"With the nephews?" she pressed.

"With Eli Kingston."

"Oh." She frowned. "Why would you do that?"

"It's a long story and it's not for fourth graders." I didn't smile, but I thought I was holding it together pretty well for a girl—sorry, *woman* as of this morning—who had been devastated earlier that day.

"Well, hold on," she said. "I thought we were going to celebrate your birthday together, but fine. Ditch me."

"I'm not ditching you," I said in exasperation.

"It's all right," she said airily, sliding off the stool at the kitchen island. "You, stay there."

Her sneakers squeaked against the hardwood floors as she crossed the kitchen and disappeared into the dining room. I leaned over the island, trying to see where she'd gone.

"You worry me," I said.

"I'm not going to light myself on fire!"

That brought me to my feet, out of the stool, so fast that I grabbed the edge of the island to steady myself. "Maddie!"

She popped her head back into the kitchen, grinning mischievously. She had one hand cupped around a cupcake to protect the candle and its flickering flame. "What? I'm practically old enough to smoke. Half the fifth grade does."

"Do not start with me," I said. "It has been a long day and I am very low on sense-of-humor."

"You definitely shouldn't go out with Eli then," she said, carefully carrying the cupcake into the room. "Cause he's a total joke."

"Well, I'm stuck." I realized as soon as the words were out of my mouth that I shouldn't have said that. Maddie didn't need to worry about my grown-up problems.

Maddie let that pass, because she began to sing, "Happy birthday."

She set the cupcake in front of me as she finished singing. I had to resist the temptation to join in, since one person singing happy birthday sounds a little sad. Instead, I eyed the cupcake: chocolate with vanilla frosting and an abundance of rainbow sprinkles. Someone knew what kind of cupcake I liked best.

"Make a wish!" she said cheerfully.

I closed my eyes, just for a second, shutting out my sister's happy face, the colorful cupcake, the orange wisp of flame above a white candle. The wish that rose up in my chest was a powerful thing, a prayer.

Save us.

I opened my eyes and blew out the candle. Maddie clapped, the sound sharp in the quiet of the room, and then I pulled out the candle and set it on the side of the plate.

"When did you get the chance to make cupcakes?" I peeled the pink cupcake wrapper away from the moist crumbs of cake.

"I didn't," she said. "Misty dropped them off while you were in the shower. She knew it was your birthday."

"Yeah," I said softly. Misty's birthday would be tomorrow. Our birthdays were so close, but our celebrations would be nothing alike: her parents always woke her with a birthday cake and presents in bed, took her to her favorite restaurant, gave her a party. I'd been to a variety of Misty's birthday parties over the year: tea parties, gymnastics parties, a horseback riding party at the local stables, our first big boy-girl party where no one danced despite an optimistic DJ. That had been the last time Misty invited me; our friendship was already weakening, but she'd invited me one last time for nostalgia's sake, I guess.

"That was kind of her," I said, belatedly. "She's always been so thoughtful."

Maddie snorted, but that was all she said about that. Maybe one day, she would grow into bullshit, but for now, she didn't have much interest in polite lies.

"I should get ready for my date," I said.

"Since when do you care what you look like for Eli?" Maddie said, and then her eyes sharpened in a way that didn't seem at all appropriate for a nine-year-old.

"Well, got to go." I wasn't interested in pursuing that line of conversation. But I couldn't quite bring myself to duck out entirely. I was worried about Maddie's tendency to eat too much sugar then end up unable to sleep, coming into my room where she kicked me all night long in her sugar-inspired nightmares. "How many cupcakes were there? Don't eat all of them."

"You can't say *don't eat all of them* without even knowing how many cupcakes there are."

"How many are there?"

I headed for the stairs, and she followed me.

"I'll tell you if you tell me who you're really dressing up for." Her voice was teasing.

I ran up the stairs without looking back. "It's the nephews."

"I knew it!"

"Don't tell anyone."

"You don't tell anyone about all those cupcakes I'm about to eat."

"Maddie!"

In my room, I combed my hair and put in earrings. I started to pat concealer over the black-and-blue bruises that marked my stubborn chin and ran up the side of my face, vivid across my cheekbone. But it caked over the bruise, turning it green instead of making it less-hideous, so I ran hot water and gently washed it off.

I was bruised, almost broken, and there was no point in trying to hide it. I was who I was. For some reason, those bruises attracted Eli, who wanted someone to hurt more.

And for some reason, those bruises drew in the strange men who'd suddenly entwined themselves in my life, even as they tried to stay away from me.

I gazed at myself in the mirror, tucking my hair behind my ears. I wasn't going to hide the bruises or fake smiles.

"Happy eighteenth birthday," I said softly to myself. Some birthday.

I couldn't bring myself to say *happy birthday, Piper*. Kai wasn't wrong. The name I'd worn all my life suddenly felt awkward, strange on my tongue, as if it wasn't supposed to be my name at all.

But I didn't have another name I'd chosen, or even the chance to grow into a new name yet. That would have to wait until I escaped.

Somehow, someday.

My cell phone dinged with a text message. Eli. Before I could even read it, a car honked outside.

I rolled my eyes—well, maybe Maddie got her annoying habits from me—and threw my cell phone into my purse as I ran downstairs.

"Bye, Maddie!" I called. My dad was coming in the door as I reached the entryway.

He nodded hello, but his gaze lingered on the bruises on my face. "Happy birthday, Piper. Aren't you going to do your makeup before you go out?"

"Thanks, Dad," I said. "I wasn't going to...hey, Eli said there's a party after the game. Is it okay if I go?"

"No drinking," he warned.

"Of course not."

"And if Eli drinks, get a ride home with someone else or call me." His gaze softened. "I'll pick you up if you need me."

"Thanks, Dad," I said again.

Once, things like that used to really confuse me—how could my father seem like he cared sometimes, and be so harsh at others? He taught me to ride a bike; he bragged about me to his friends; he told me I was pretty.

Maybe that was why people got so confused, thinking it must be okay to hurt kids. Parents' love seemed so complicated.

Eli honked the horn again. I winced.

"Your boyfriend is a dickhead," he said frankly.

It made me smile, and I touched the split in my lip, which was healing but ached when I smiled suddenly like that. "I don't know if I'd go all the way to *boyfriend*. It's one date."

"Well, good luck." He headed into the house.

"Curfew?" I called after him, wanting to make sure I didn't do something to get myself in trouble without even knowing.

"Whenever you want to tell him," Dad called back. "Whatever you can stand."

Happy birthday to me, indeed.

"Oh hey," Dad said, turning back. "I won't hold you back now, but I have a birthday present for you. Birthday breakfast tomorrow?"

"That would be nice."

"I'll take you to Frenchy's," he promised. "Make sure you and Maddie are ready at nine."

And despite everything, I felt guilty when I said goodnight and closed the door between us.

Being alone—like the judge had pointed out I was, over and over, so very helpfully—was hard. But I didn't think anything could be as hard as trying to figure out other people.

16

Eli took me to the local coffee shop on our way to the football game. As he parked in the lot, he said, "I hate that I have to leave you for the game. But at least you can have something hot to drink. It's going to be cold in the bleachers tonight."

"Thanks," I said.

"White chocolate mocha, right?" When he pushed the door open for me, the bells chimed and a blast of pleasantly warm air rushed out.

"You know me," I said.

"What do I drink?" he asked, a playful note in his voice.

I had no idea. "Before a game? I would think you'd stick with Gatorade."

"Normally," he clarified. He took my hand and led me through the warm, vanilla-scented coffee shop to the counter. "You're a white chocolate mocha and I'm..."

"Iced coffee?"

He shot me a disappointed look. To the barista at the counter, he said, "We'll take a white chocolate mocha, and I'm just going to grab a Gatorade from the case."

I kept my eye-rolling internal. He paid, and then caught the sleeve of my coat, tugging me toward him as he stepped backward toward the other end of the counter.

"I guess you've never been that interested in me," he said, his voice cool. "I've always noticed stuff about you."

"I'm not that observant," I lied. "What is it that you like?"

His lips pursed. He was really a good-looking guy, his lips nicely-shaped over a determined jaw. It was his personality that made his face so unattractive to me I could barely stand to look at him. I turned my back, running my fingertips over the ceramic travel mugs that lined the shelves.

"Half-coffee, half-espresso, one pump of simple syrup," he said, his voice low over my shoulder, just before his hand pressed against my stomach, holding me against his waist. "It's a little bit bitter, with just a tease of sweet."

"And here I would have figured you for a frappe guy."

I didn't know why I couldn't keep my mouth shut. I froze for a second, gauging his reaction, but he smiled. The tightness in my chest eased.

"I don't like things too sweet," he said, his voice a fevered whisper; it felt as if his breath scraped my ear. I hated being this close to him.

"White chocolate mocha," the barista called, setting the cup down on the counter. She smiled at him. "Have a good game, Mr. Kingston."

"Thank you." He released me and when I turned around, he held my drink out, an indulgent smile playing across his lips. "You have a sweet tooth, though, don't you? You're basically drinking caffeinated hot chocolate."

"It's delicious," I defended my drink, taking it from him.

The barista watched us curiously as she returned to the espresso machine, and I wondered what she saw. I bet to a casual observer, Eli seemed charming and affectionate. I probably looked like a lucky girl.

At the football game, I climbed into the still-almost empty

bleachers and sat down, wrapping my hands around the cardboard cup to keep my drink warm as long as I could. Eli was right; it was chilly in the bleachers. There'd been a steady wind all day, the cool held at bay by the sun, but now the wind blew right through my jacket.

I wasn't used to coming out to football games, and I shifted on the cold metal seat. A few adults came and sat down in front of me—someone's parents—and they were so warmly dressed and bearing so much stuff they could barely maneuver down the aisle. They unloaded thermoses, seat cushions, and blankets, setting up like they were going to be here all night.

"Hey." Nick scooted in the aisle until he stood next to me. His walk seemed off, as if he was putting more weight on one leg than the other, but it was hard to tell when he was negotiating the narrow aisle. "You mind if I sit here?"

Although I desperately wanted to sit with Nick, I should be honest. "My date probably does."

His head jerked up. "Who's your date?"

"Eli Kingston."

"Oh, he's in the game. You sitting with friends?"

I shook my head.

"You are now." He had a backpack over his shoulder, and he pitched it to the ground between us before he sat next to me. For a few seconds, we sat in silence, watching the football players warming up on the field.

Eli looked up at me to wave as they were exiting the field, and when he saw Nick, he frowned.

I waved back, pretending I didn't notice the expression that crossed his face. A spike of guilt jolted me, though. I should at least be respectful if I was going to humor him by going on this stupid date.

Or did I ever really have a choice? I remembered Eli's victorious gaze as my father grilled me in the entryway, as my father volunteered me for this date, and my guilt dropped away. I might pay later with Eli's sullen silence—and I knew he'd hurt me, one day, if he got the chance—but for now, I had three hours to spend with a boy I actually liked to talk to.

"Have Kai and Josh been playing since they were kids?" I asked.

"Hmm?" He made an absent noise, and then said, "Oh, yeah. I guess they have."

"Not your thing?"

"Definitely not my thing."

"Are you not a team sports guy?"

"I spend enough time with a *team*," he said. "Did you see all the testosterone in that house?"

"I did." All that shirtless, hard-angled, handsome testosterone. Not that I'd noticed. Nick, with his broad shoulders and chiseled jaw, seemed like he fit into that world just fine, so I was curious what was going on under the surface.

I shivered, and Nick's eyes widened. "You cold?"

"I'm fine," I said, but he was already unbuttoning the wool peacoat he wore. He slipped it off and threw it over my shoulders.

"You're going to freeze," I chided him.

"Nah," he said. "I run warm. I don't really need it."

"You and your brother both," I said, and then there was an awkward pause between us while I wondered why I'd just brought up Josh.

"Speaking of the devil," he said, nodding at the field as the Blissford Wolves surged onto the field.

We watched in silence as the game began. Eli started; Kai and Josh warmed the bench. Across from us, the cheerleaders had to be freezing in their skirts. The mascot, a small guy wearing an enormous gray wolf's head that made him seem like he was stumbling around top-heavy, waved from the sidelines.

"You guys must feel comfortable here," I said, thinking of Callum's wolfish art. "Wolves everywhere."

Nick turned to me in surprise, his lips parting, then shrugged. "I guess Blissford used to have a lot of wolves in the mountains."

Eli ran hard with the ball, finding a path through the opposing team. The crowd jumped to their feet around us, as if their energy could spur him faster. When he got sacked, he held onto the ball and bobbed up to his feet, raising it above his head. The crowd cheered for him.

"Now they're just here in the student body," I joked.

Nick's eyes seemed to follow mine. The faint lines around his hard-angled mouth were suddenly etched more deeply, making him look older. "I guess so."

"You guess a lot of things," I teased.

He leaned back, bracing his elbow on his knee, so he could look at me in the face when we sat so close together. His face changed in an instant, suddenly transforming into light-hearted, handsome flirtation. "Oh, there's plenty that I know."

"Yeah? What's that?"

"I know that being really good at something like, say, football may make people like you, but it doesn't mean you're actually *good*," he said. "I know that nice people sometimes miss what's right in front of them because they think everyone else is just like them."

The look he gave me was meaningful.

I patted his knee, being purposefully just as condescending as he was. "Trust me, nice doesn't mean stupid. *Nice* people can see plenty."

"And yet here we are," he said.

"Here I am, sitting next to you," I retorted. I started to move my hand from his leg, but he rested his hand on mine.

"Your hands are cold," he murmured, his thumb tracing back and forth across my palm.

I leaned in, close to him, and he ducked his ear toward my lips.

"I'm on a date with another boy," I said softly, "and you just took my hand. Could you be any more cocky?"

He turned his face into my hair, and I tilted my head, curious what he would whisper back.

"You're on a date with another boy, and you're holding my hand."

I shook my head. "You started it."

"Just trying to warm you up." He cupped my hand in his, raising it to his lips to blow on my fingers. His breath, and the grip of his big hands, was warm, and it did feel good on my cold skin.

"I know things too," I said, gently pulling my hand out of his. "I know trouble when I see it."

"Yeah?"

"You and your brothers," I said, "you're trouble."

"Good trouble," he promised me.

"No such thing."

He shrugged, a lazy rise of one big shoulder. "Agree to disagree. We'll re-evaluate later when you've gotten the chance to know us better."

"Cocky," I confirmed.

"Nah."

The smile that played across his lips was sexy as hell, and even though I'd just pushed him away, it made me fantasize about pulling him close.

He reached into his backpack and pulled out a pair of thick, fleece-lined leather gloves. He held the first one open for me to slip my hand into.

"You had these the whole time and you just wanted to torment my would-be boyfriend?" I raised an eyebrow at him, but slipped my hand into the welcoming warm fleece.

"Okay," he admitted, "sometimes I *am* just trouble. I don't like that guy. And I wouldn't mind stealing you away from him."

"It wouldn't be stealing," I said hotly. "I'm not a *thing*. I can't be stolen."

His lips tightened. I thought he was mad, and for a second, silence reigned between us. I stared out at the field, watching players rearrange themselves.

"You're right," he said. "I'm sorry. I didn't think about what I was saying."

The apology startled me. "Oh. It's okay."

"And it's not him I care about." He bumped his shoulder against mine, flashing me a meaningful look.

"You barely even know me."

He inclined his head. "I guess I can't argue with that."

I tried to hide the grin that came to my lips. I didn't want to hurt his feelings, but he had said *I guess* eighteen times in this conversation.

"What?" he asked.

I raised my eyebrows at him innocently over my cup and took a long sip, avoiding the conversation.

"They're sending in Josh and Kai," he said, bumping my shoulder with his. The light-hearted contact sent warmth flooding through my arm.

"At the same time? Bold move. Since no one knows how good they really are."

Nick's gorgeous green eyes studied me. For a second, they reminded me of someone I knew, although I couldn't place who. He promised, "They're good."

Josh and Kai seemed as if they knew what the other one was thinking, and they made a successful run up the field. Josh had the ball and Kai ran alongside him. People jumped to their feet around us as, with the opposing side knotting up around them, Kai and Josh almost seemed to collide.

Then Josh burst out of the pack, dragging two players behind him. Kai flipped over the back of one of the opposing players and ran hard for the goal. It took a second for all of us to see clearly. Kai had the ball!

He ran across the goal lines and then turned around by the goal posts. The cheering around me was thunderous, but Kai's expression under the bright lights seemed confused for a second, as if he was double checking that he had done the right thing. Then he raised his hand, waving to the crowd, as he tucked the ball under his arm.

The team flooded around Josh and Kai. Eli looked up to me, and the expression on his face was thunderous. I gave him an encouraging smile and a wave.

Then, with the noise and chaos blocking any eavesdroppers, I leaned over to Nick. "Does Kai know how to play football?"

He froze, almost imperceptibly, before he smiled. "Doesn't it look like he does?"

"Yeah. It *looks* like."

There was no doubt in my mind that there was something weird about these guys.

Nick shrugged instead of answering.

Something weird, but something wonderful too.

17

"Great game," I said to Eli. We stood at the edge of the parking lot. The Wolves had won.

Josh and Kai were surrounded by a group of teenagers, on their way to the car—the parking lot was noisy and filled with people—but Josh stood almost head-and-shoulders above the crowd. He was a big guy, despite the leanness of his muscle. His gaze ran idly through the crowd until his eyes met mine. His eyes locked on mine.

"Yeah." Eli sounded as thrilled as he would if they lost. "Well, let's get going."

He put his arm around my shoulders, his posture protective, and glared at Josh. Josh stared at him, his expression completely neutral and composed. Deep blue eyes watched us go as Eli pulled me toward the car.

It was only when we were in the car, with the heat blasting, that Eli said, "You sat with the new guy."

"Well, he sat with me," I said. "I was already there."

"Free country," Eli said.

"That's right."

"And you're a friendly girl." There was a faint bitterness in his voice, and I had the sense of simmering anger under the surface.

"I try to be nice to everyone," I said. Saying the word *nice* made me think about conversations I'd had recently with Kai and with Nick. *I don't owe you anything. Nice people don't see what's right in front of them.*

"You're not that nice to me, Piper."

I glanced at my mirror, at the parking lot full of people we were leaving behind. "Where's the party at?"

Headlights glowed in my mirror, momentarily dazzling me, and I glanced back at Eli's face in profile. His lips pressed together.

"Our lake house," he said. "I guess we have to go."

"Your parents don't mind?"

He didn't bother to answer.

But he did pick up the prior line of conversation, the one I'd hoped he would drop. "You were a little nicer to the new guy than you needed to be, weren't you?"

"I'm just being friendly, Eli. Like to everyone new in school." I said it firmly, trying to shut down as much of an argument as I could.

His fingers flexed on the steering wheel. "All right."

He turned his truck into the driveway. There were already a few cars parked in the driveway, but he maneuvered around them and hit the button on the rearview mirror. A completely empty concrete bay loomed in front of us.

He pulled in, and the garage door rumbled shut behind us. I sat stiffly for a few long seconds, anxious about being alone with him.

But he released his seat belt and came around and opened the door for me before I could get out. His smile seemed stiff, but like he was trying.

He opened the door from the garage to the house. "Come on in. Do you want a drink?"

"I'm all right," I said. Imagining my instincts relaxing, the tension that kept me coiled up and uncomfortable but also safe, around Eli made me uncomfortable. "Thank you."

He shrugged and led me into the house. We entered a big, Pinterest-worthy kitchen, with an iced keg sitting on the tile at the end of the island. "Your parents want you to have a party?" I asked.

"You're only young once, my dad says." Eli picked a red Solo cup from a stack. "I'm pretty sure he'd go back to high school if he could."

"Life doesn't seem so bad for him now," I said.

"What about your dad?" Eli asked, before taking a long sip of his beer. Foam flecked his upper lip, and he licked it off.

I crinkled my nose. I didn't want to talk about my father tonight.

"He's just kind of a mystery," Eli said. "Moved here out of nowhere, bought the plant when no one thought the McGuires would sell, mysterious wife…"

"You wouldn't remember my mom," I said. "Of course she'd be mysterious."

I didn't even remember my mother, but I didn't like Eli talking about her.

"Not me," he said. "My dad and I were talking about it."

There was a pile of chips and pretzels in bags at the end of the island, and I set to opening the crinkly bags and rolling down the tops, just to give myself something to do. It was strange to think about Eli and his dad chatting about my father. I tried to imagine the context. Was it about Eli and me dating? Or because Eli's dad coveted my father's power, wishing he could consolidate the two factories—and gain complete control of the town?

"That reminds me," he said. "I've got a gift for you. Happy birthday, Piper."

"Your dad reminded you it's my birthday?" I said, trying to make my voice teasing.

He nodded. "Come upstairs with me."

Down the hall, the doorbell rang. Impatiently, he ran and wrenched the front door open. "Yeah, hi, make yourself at home."

"I don't know," I said as he passed me, grabbing my wrist and towing me behind him toward the dark wooden stairs. "My father's rules definitely include staying out of boys' rooms."

"Your father has a lot of rules for you." His fingers were still tight on my arm. "You ever wonder why?"

"He's just a control freak."

"Yeah. My dad says he says you can't be trusted to make your own decisions."

"Great." I knew when my ego was being played—I was sure Eli was trying to manipulate me now, into rebelling against my father by doing whatever he wanted—but I didn't much care for the idea of my father discussing my so-called flaws around the poker table.

"I don't believe that, Piper," he said, glancing over his shoulder at me. For once, there was a spark of kindness in his eyes. "Your father's full of shit."

Strange that Eli was right twice in one night.

"We're not going to do anything," he said, stopping in front of a bedroom door, his hand on the knob. "I promise, Piper."

That promise sounded less like a *we aren't going to do anything* and more like *I'm not going to do anything to you.*

Eli seemed to know my fears, and even though he reassured me, he had to know that I questioned going anywhere with him. I wondered what was going through his head.

He pushed open the door and walked in ahead of me, then picked up a small, silvery-wrapped gift from the foot of the bed. He held it out to me, a smile on his face.

"I hope you like it," he said.

I hurried to unwrap it. The sooner I opened his gift, the sooner we could go back downstairs into the crowd. Even from here, with the door to the room standing open, I could hear voices and laughter beginning to fill the house downstairs.

I pulled off the wrapping paper, and inside was a long blue jewelry box. I glanced up at Eli. His gaze was intent on my face, a smile on his lips.

"Open it," he said. "Don't be shy."

A beautiful silver-and-sapphire necklace lay inside. When I touched the jewels, they slid over my fingers, heavy and cool. "It's so pretty." I looked up at him, confused. This was an expensive gift. "I don't understand."

"What's not to understand?" He took the box out of my hand and gestured to indicate I should spin. "Beautiful jewelry for a beautiful girl."

I turned around, running my fingers through my long blond hair and pulling it up on top of my head in a loose bun. As he slipped the necklace around my neck, I caught a glimpse of us in the mirror that hung alongside his door. He was tall and handsome, his gaze on me hungry. With my hands drawing up my hair from my slender neck and the elaborate jewelry against my throat, I looked pretty—and blank. I stared into the mirror like I was lost in a daydream. Someone who saw us would think, once again, *what a lucky girl.*

I blinked, coming back to life, and shook my hair out over my shoulders. "Thank you."

"You're welcome." He tucked his hand into his pocket, looking over me consideringly. "Come on. I told my dad we'd tell him how the game went, and how you liked your present, before we got too busy with the party."

"Your dad?"

"He likes you," he said, holding out his hand to me.

"That's a change," I said, hiding a smile.

"He's always liked you."

The sheer amount of time we had spent discussing his daddy and his daddy's expectations tonight was beginning to make me think something was awry.

"Does your dad want us to date?" I asked softly. Maybe Eli's stupid crush was all a cover for learning more about my family.

"I don't want to date you, Piper." A perplexed look crossed his face.

I met his gaze, frowning. "We're on a date right now."

"I thought you got it," he said, setting his cup down so he could take my face in his hands.

I froze, adrenaline suddenly coursing through my legs.

A slow, arrogant smirk twisted across Eli's lips. "I don't want to date you. I want to *own* you."

"I'm not a thing," I told him, echoing what I'd said to Nick earlier. I wrapped my fingers around his wrists, pulling his grip away from my face, but his fingers curled painfully around my face, his fingertips sinking into my cheekbones.

His breath was a hot flutter against my ear. "You're not a person, either."

I pushed him away from me as hard as I could, and he slammed into the pool table. I ran for the door, but he didn't chase me.

Behind me, he laughed, a hard, mean sound.

"Good luck running, Piper."

I didn't break my stride. I ran down the hall, barreled frantically down the stairs. My purse slammed against my side as I ran into the crowd. My dad, I'd call my dad to pick me up. I had to get away from Eli.

What a *creep*. I'd known he was a creep, but he was an even weirder creep than I thought.

I shoved into someone's back as I was rushing through the crowd, and he turned around. Josh loomed in front of me. The beer that had been in his hand was all over his t-shirt. When our eyes met, he said, "Hey. Are you okay?"

Despite myself, I grabbed his tattooed forearm. My heart pounded so hard it ached in my chest. I looked up at him and nodded. I didn't trust my voice.

"Come here," he said softly, catching my hand against his arm. He pulled me away from the crowd, into the quiet of the hallway.

"I've got to get out of here," I whispered.

"I'll take you home," he said without hesitation.

I wanted to throw myself against his chest. I longed for him to wrap his arms around me. It felt like he could protect me from Eli.

But could he, really? Should I trust him when I barely knew him?

My lips parted, on the verge of asking him to wait with me while I called my father.

Misty shoved out of the crowd. Her face was alight, her soft brown curls blowing back from her face. She looked lovely and glowing.

"There you are," she said to Josh. Her eyes flickered to me, and the faintest frown line dimpled over the bridge of her nose. Her gaze returned to him. "I've been looking for you. You promised me that dance!"

"Later, Misty," he said. "I have to take care of something."

She bit down on her lower lip, obviously hurt, but smiled anyway as she shrugged. "All right."

"I'm sorry," he said to her, and it sounded like he meant it for more than the moment's disruption. He took my hand in his and tugged me gently toward the front door.

Outside on the front porch, I drew in a breath of cool air. For the first time, I realized I was feverishly hot, on the verge of sweating. My head swam.

"Piper," Josh said, catching me by the elbows. His worried face blurred before my eyes. "What's wrong?"

"I don't know."

"Did you drink anything?" Those vibrant blue eyes were all I could see, even though his sexy, urgent voice seemed distant.

"No." I shook my head. "Can you just wait with me while I call my dad? Then you can go back to the party. Back to Misty."

I was too sick to hide the bitter inflection when I said Misty's name. I shook my head, trying to clear my bad attitude away, and the headache too. God. She used to be my friend, and she was still trying to be. Those cupcakes were the act of a sweet soul, the girl I knew before she was caught up in her popularity. She still *was* sweet, even though she'd abandoned our stupid, childhood plots to escape my father and then she'd begun to ignore me most of the time. I should be happy for her.

"Stay with me," Josh muttered. He was still frowning as he tucked my hair behind my ear. "I'll bring you home, but I want to bring you home with me."

I cocked my head at him. "But Misty?"

"Don't be stupid," he said, his voice rougher than I'd heard it before. "I'm fucking that all up, aren't I? But I can't pretend."

"Why would you pretend?"

He shook his head, refusing to answer. "Can I take you to see Callum, before I take you home? You don't seem…right."

"Neither do you." My teasing words came out slurred. I stopped, perplexed.

Nick burst out onto the porch, followed by Kai. "What's up?"

My vision went dark around the edges. As I swayed, Josh caught me around my waist, and my cheek settled against his hard chest. Warm arms wrapped around me.

"This is exactly what I was trying to avoid," I muttered, even though it'd also been exactly what I wanted, despite the reasonable part of my brain.

"I've got you," Josh promised. His arm slid under my thighs and he picked me up, easily lifting me against his chest.

Wrapped in his warmth and the spicy, pleasant scent of his cologne, my brain itself hot and aching, I fell helplessly into sleep.

18

Opening my eyes seemed impossible. My head ached and my eyelids were so heavy I couldn't imagine waking up.

"Put her on the couch," Callum said, his voice calm and urgent all at once. "What happened to her?"

Josh still cradled me in his arms as he sat with me, his big palm tenderly cupping my face to hold my head against his shoulder. "I don't know. But I'm pretty sure Eli Kingston did something to her."

His voice was gravelly with rage.

"Calm down," Callum said. "We can wait for the story." Cool hands touched my face, then Callum said, "She's burning up. Josh, I'm not kidding—put her *down* on the couch. I need space to work."

Josh grumbled, but got up with me, before shifting me gently onto the couch.

"You could bring her downstairs," Nick said.

"That's just what we need, for her to wake up in a makeshift operating room," Callum said. "Might be hard to explain, huh?"

His fingers brushed against my throat, then tightened around the necklace. "What the hell is this?"

"I haven't seen it before," Josh said.

"She wasn't wearing it tonight," Nick said.

"You would've noticed?" Kai asked.

"Yeah," Nick said frankly. "I would have noticed."

Callum tried to wrench the necklace away, and pain seared through my body. I groaned as every muscle spasmed, tightening like a terrible Charlie horse. My eyes flew open, my lips parting as the groan almost became a scream.

"What did you do to her?" Nick sounded as though he was about to shove Callum out of the way.

Callum's eyes locked on mine. "What did you do, Piper? What is this?"

As my muscles relaxed, I fell back into the couch. My head still ached desperately. I tried to tell him I didn't know, but the words came out as a croak.

"It's enchanted," Callum muttered. "Someone bound her. Or she chose to bind herself to someone…"

"Eli." Nick said. "He bound her. To take away her will?"

"I'm going to fucking kill him," Josh said. He headed for the door.

"Stop," Callum called, his voice sharp. Josh didn't break stride.

Callum nodded to Kai, and Kai went after Josh.

"Hang on." Callum ordered. "We need to figure out exactly what happened, where guilt lies, and then develop a plan. You can't go after the witch without a plan—"

"Got a plan," Josh whipped back over his shoulder. "I'm going to rip off Eli's head."

"Be right back," Callum said, jumping to his feet. I lost sight of him, because my head was too heavy to lift with my aching neck, but I heard Kai slam into Josh, trying to stop him, and then a thud as Callum joined the fray.

Nick sighed, leaning into my line of vision. His fingertips brushed my cheekbones. "I'm on Josh's side, here."

"You can't go around ripping people's heads off." My voice came out gravelly, but at least it was audible this time.

"It's time the real wolves ruled Blissford again," he muttered, "not the football team."

"Wolves?" I asked, perplexed.

Nick smiled, leaning forward. He had a nice, warm smile, and I could get lost in those deep green eyes.

"You're dreaming, sweetheart," he said softly, running his fingertips over my forehead. "It's just part of the fever."

"As long as I'm dreaming." I caught his hand, feeling a surge of warmth and energy when he touched me. Enlivened, just a little, I pulled his hand to my lips.

Interest sparked in his eye. Or maybe that was lust that joined the warm compassion and concern. I kissed the inside of his palm, watching his face. When my lips brushed against his palm, his eyes drifted halfway shut, as if that smallest tender contact gave him pleasure.

"As long as none of this ever happened," he murmured.

A *thud* sounded in the entryway behind me, followed by a sharp curse.

"Just another dream of mine," I said, and his eyes widened. Shit. I'd given away a bit too much with that revelation. *Blame my foggy brain.*

I parted my lips, trying to figure out a way to downplay the truth I'd accidentally let slip, and he leaned forward and kissed me.

His kiss was gentle, tentative. His fingers wrapped around mine, and he held my hand as his lips brushed softly over my mouth. I kissed him, back.

Callum was back, breathing hard, standing behind Nick. He crossed his arms and sighed. "Out of my way. The three of you are hopeless."

Josh glowered at him. A trickle of blood stained the left corner of his lip.

Nick squeezed my hand and gave me an encouraging smile before he stood, moving aside so Callum could kneel next to me again. "Don't mind Callum. He's all bark."

"I've got some bite too," Callum promised, his eyes cool. "I am the head of this...house." His gaze flickered to Josh, and then to me. "Taking care of everyone in it isn't always fun for any of us."

"You're an asshole," Josh said.

"And you went feral without a pack," Callum said. "But you'll learn."

I stared at them, feeling like if only my head didn't ache, this would all make sense.

Kai sighed. "I'm the only one who can keep a secret around here, huh?"

"She won't remember," Callum said. He ran his hand over my forehead, his touch comforting. "I can't do anything to release the enchantment now, Piper. It will take time—and the blood of the witch who set up the magic. But we'll get you free, and we'll watch over you in the meantime."

"Eli must have known there was only one way he could get her in his bed," Kai muttered, his voice full of fury.

"He gave me the necklace," I said softly. "I didn't know. Enchantments? Wolves? What's going on?"

"Meet the last of the Blissford pack," Callum said. "Well, most of it. We're werewolves, Piper."

"Werewolves," I said softly.

"Something was stolen from us seventeen years ago," Callum said. "We've come home to get it back. You're on pack land, our land for hundreds of years."

"Werewolves," I repeated.

Callum glanced at his 'nephews', as if to point out how fever-damaged my brain was at the moment.

"You're safe on pack land," he promised me, "and you always will be."

"I have to get home," I said.

He shook his head. "Impossible. We can't explain what happened to your father, and someone needs to watch over you all night. The enchantment has its claws in you now, and if we try to break it while it's still bonding with your body..."

"What'll happen?" Nick demanded.

"It doesn't matter," Callum said. "In the morning, we'll get Eli to pay for his sins. We'll break the enchantment."

His fingers skimmed my face, regret changing his face. "Then we'll have to make you forget. It's the only way to protect you, and to protect ourselves."

"No," Josh said. "You can't do that to her."

"It won't hurt," Callum said. Sharply, he added, "I've had enough of you tonight. You've put everything at risk."

"I didn't do this," Josh said hotly. "What did you want me to do? Leave her there as prey?"

"No," Callum said. "Of course not."

"I can't stay here overnight," I said. "My father will be looking for me. He'll kill me."

"He won't," Callum promised. "We'll protect you."

"Good luck," I muttered. "No one else will. Happy eighteenth birthday to me."

Behind Callum, Kai and Josh shared a meaningful look. Nick's deep green eyes were still fixed on me.

"We owe you," Nick said.

Callum said, "Nick. No."

"You have my bond," Nick said. "No one's going to hurt you as long as I'm alive."

Callum rubbed his hand across his face. "You three have a lot to learn about being part of a pack."

"What did I do?" Kai demanded.

"You're as bad as the other two."

I raised my hands, about to demand an explanation, but I was almost too exhausted to move. As my hands fell, I caught Callum's wrist. He turned to me, frowning, as my fingers wrapped tight around his wrist. His eyes met mine, and he didn't pull away.

"We'll take turns keeping watch over her tonight," Callum said to them. "If her condition changes during your watch, wake me."

He stood, taking away his warmth and his comforting solidity. As he stood over me, his eyes studied my face, as if I were a puzzle he couldn't quite make sense of.

"Kai, you take first watch," Callum said. "I have some business to tend."

Kai nodded, and he knelt beside the couch, taking Callum's place.

"All of you," Callum said roughly. "She needs rest. Keep your hands to yourselves. You can't keep drawing a tighter and tighter bond with the wrong goddamn girl."

The three of them exchanged a glance as Callum headed for the door. It was only when he'd shut it behind him that Josh muttered something, his tone rebellious.

I was falling back into sleep, but his words still lodged in my mind.

"Maybe fate's a lie," he had said.

19

I slept fitfully, and when I opened my eyes again, Kai was watching over me. His lips flickered in a faint smile, as if welcoming me back into the world, before he said, "Go back to sleep, girl."

I scrambled up onto my elbows, shaking sleep from my foggy head. The lights were off in the living room except for a lamp in the corner, by the bookcases, and the glow of the fire in the fireplace.

I shivered, hard, suddenly as deeply bone-cold as I'd been fever-hot. Kai stood and leaned over me as he pulled a blanket up over my legs. His tattooed arms and lean muscles stood out as he tucked the blanket under my thighs, his touch firm and caring. Then he sat on the edge of the couch, rubbing my arm with his hand as if to warm me. "Better?"

"I can't be here," I said softly. I tried to sort through my blurry memories of the night for how I'd ended up in this particular moment. I knew it made sense that I was here, but I couldn't remember all the details. "My father…"

"…is not someone you have to worry about," Kai said firmly. "Callum'll have a talk with him."

I shook my head. "You don't know who my father is. He's powerful in this town."

Kai's thumb traced across my forearm in gentle circles, as if comforting me. "So are we. Or at least, we could be."

"Charming the school and winning over the football team?" I asked, my eyebrows arching. "I'm not sure I'd call that *power*."

Kai shrugged. "I'd prefer to avoid attention, but I was outvoted."

"You don't like attention." It wasn't a question.

"Depends on who it's from," he said offhandedly.

I put my hand over his, and he shook his head, leaning away. "You've got to rest. And I have strict orders to be on my best behavior."

"What do you think I was going to do?" I asked, mock innocently.

He leveled a bossy look at me that was surprisingly adorable. "I think we both know damn well that sparks fly whenever you and I are close. But you took the magic equivalent of a blow to the head and the flu all at once, so just lie there and go," he leaned forward to brush his lips over my forehead, kisses punctuating each word, "back, to, sleep."

"Magic is real," I murmured.

"Magic is real," he said, his eyes worried. I tried to take his shoulders in my hands, but he ducked out of my grip, too quick to catch, although some of the worry was chased away. A playful smile twisted his lips. "And you seem to be magic yourself, girl."

"I'm not anything," I said, some of my memories of the night before returning. "But you're a...wolf."

"Now and then." He ran his hand over my leg, through the blanket, his touch warming me like nothing else.

"Hold me," I said. "I'm warm when you're near me."

His lips twisted, in an amused smirk, although he moved to obey. Before I knew it, he lifted me easily, and my head was on his hard shoulder, his arms locked around me. I rested my cheek against the soft flannel of his shirt.

"Princess," he accused gently. Then he fell silent, as if he was thinking about something.

"What is it?" I asked.

"Something impossible," he said.

"Everything I learned about tonight is impossible," I said. "Enchanted necklaces. Binding spells. Werewolves."

His fingers traced my throat, just beneath the curve of the cold metal that seemed to bite into my skin. "You seem to be taking…this…well."

"Callum said you guys would help me get it off," I said.

"And you trust us." His big hand swept the hair from my forehead. Despite himself, and all he'd said, his lips grazed my forehead again.

"Shouldn't I?" I yawned.

"Maybe," he said softly. "But I'm glad you do. And you have my bond."

"I don't know what that is." I turned my face into his chest, letting my eyes drift shut again.

His fingers ran through my hair, sending gentle tugs of pleasure racing down my spine. "It means we'd die to protect you. It means we'll always come when you need us."

"That's crazy talk," I muttered. "No one's going to die."

"Eli Kingston just might," Kai said, his voice bleak.

We'll always come when you need us.

They were sweet words to think over while I fell into sleep.

When I woke again, Nick held me in his arms. I stared up at his big jaw, those beautiful green eyes.

Beautiful green eyes.

The limp.

I bit down on my lower lip as he smiled down at me.

"Go back to sleep, sweet girl. I've got you."

"I hit you with my car," I said flatly.

"It wasn't your fault." He tucked a strand of hair back behind my ear. "I was out of control. The werewolf thing…it's a bit new to me."

"Why's that?"

"It starts around eighteen for most males," he said. "I had my birthday a few months ago. Right after Callum finally tracked me down."

"What happened to you guys?" I asked.

"I don't remember any of it, really," he said. "I was just a baby. A coven attacked our pack and destroyed our pack. Callum was barely a teenager. He had to take the cubs—Kai, Josh and me—and run. We were the only survivors. Well, we thought."

"Who else survived?"

"There was a brand-new girl baby." His eyes clouded. "They took her. A born shifter female is powerful. Her magic can be used to fuel a coven's spells."

I finally put together the pieces. Their mission. Their talk about a bond with the *right* girl. "And you're looking for her here."

He nodded.

"And you think it's... Misty." God, the thought twisted in my chest, leaving a dull ache behind. I wished I was special. I wished, most of all, that I was special to these three.

"They hid her right in town," he said. "Right under our noses. Not that any of us could look. Callum tried to keep us together, but we were scattered to foster care and adopted to different families."

"That must have been so hard," I said softly.

"I didn't know anything else," he said. "I didn't know I had another family. All this." He jerked his chin, encompassing the big house, the estate. "It's almost everything I ever wanted."

"What's the other thing?"

His lips pursed to one side, and he shook his head. He wasn't going to answer.

"Misty," I said softly. "Your...mate? Is that how it works?"

"I don't want Misty," he said. "She's a nice girl, but I don't feel anything when I look at her. Maybe they found the wrong girl. And either way..."

"Either way, what?"

"Traditions don't matter to me," he said bluntly. "Like Callum said, we have a lot to learn about being a pack. Well, I don't care about the rules of a world I didn't grow up in. I don't want to share one *pack princess* I don't even love."

"And here I thought Kai was the bad boy type," I said softly. "Wait, share?"

He nodded, but didn't volunteer any more information. My

cheeks heated at the thought of how much I'd like to share all four of them. Even cranky, bossy Callum, with his powerful body and his distant attitude.

Actually, maybe *especially* Callum. It was inappropriate, but just thinking about him sent a spike of lust throbbing between my thighs.

Apparently, I was feeling much better.

I frowned. I finally had the chance to unravel all their secrets, and I wanted to ask every question I had. "And you and Josh are brothers?"

"No, not really," he said. "Just part of our awful cover story." He crinkled his nose at this admission. "We didn't really think it through. Callum and his *nephews*."

"Phew," I said out loud.

He cocked an eyebrow at me. "Why *phew*?"

I shook my head. I was not going to discuss the inappropriate lust-soaked thoughts that ran through my head when it came to all three of them.

"Why are you telling me all this?" I asked.

"Because you won't remember later," he said, "after the enchantment's been broken. I can finally tell you everything it's been making me crazy to hide."

"Then what?"

He groaned. "I don't know. Can we not talk about the future when it seems more than bleak right now?"

"Why would it be bleak?"

He turned exasperated eyes on me. "I don't know, why do you think fated love would feel bleak to me right now?"

"Misty's a sweetheart. And she's so pretty. You could do worse."

He growled, the sound half-animal and half lust-filled, frustrated man, and it made me grin.

"I want what I want," he said. His gaze was on my lips, and my cheeks flushed hot.

"And what is it that you want?" I asked archly. "If there were no fate? No pack?"

He took my chin in his grip, his thumb gentle against my jaw. "You know damn well."

"Maybe." I couldn't hide my grin. "I want to hear you say it."

"I want you, you brat," he said, and his lips brushed against mine.

This time, when he kissed me so tenderly, I kissed him back hard. We traded quick, frantic kisses. He kissed me like he needed me, his fingers tangling in my hair, his forearm tightening against my back, holding me tight to him. My fingertips dug into his broad, powerful shoulders, holding him against me too, making sure he wouldn't escape.

When he broke away from me, I could feel how hard he was, pressing against me through his jeans.

"I wish I could be special for you," I said softly.

"Don't you worry about being special," he said, his voice low and rough with desire. "Just be mine."

I pressed my palm against his cheek, looking into his eyes. I wanted him so badly, yet everything in that wild story said they had a pack to rebuild, something that mattered more than the crush between us. As powerful as this desire felt, he had a mission. I should be practical, and so should he. I shouldn't let my heart get too deeply twined with his.

"You know there are rules," I said. "But I'll take what I can get of you, if you'll take what you can have of me. Until you have to leave."

"Fuck the rules," he said, and he kissed me again.

We traded quick, frantic kisses. I took his big jaw in my hands, wanting to savor every bit of his mouth: the quirk at the corners, the fullness of his lower lip, the way his lips parted, welcoming me in. I ran my fingertips under his t-shirt, feeling the hard plane of his abs, the warmth of his skin, and he moaned into my mouth.

The door creaked open. Nick's lips nuzzled the corner of my mouth, and he pulled away reluctantly.

Callum came around the corner of the couch. His eyes flickered over my mussed hair and swollen-sore lips, then looked to Nick.

"Well, you *were* the one who hadn't pissed me off lately," Callum said to him. "Christ. The three of you..."

"Kai thinks there's something going on here," Nick said. "There's got to be a reason we're all drawn to Piper..."

"Just wait until the magic binding Misty is broken," Callum said. "Someone put spells on her, and when they're released, you'll see just how much power she really has."

"It's not power I'm drawn to," Nick said.

"You will be," Callum promised. "The power of the pack princess is... intense. She bonds the whole pack together."

"We're already pretty bound together," Nick said.

"You don't know," Callum said, his voice gentle. "You don't remember anything about the life we had before. But it's worth all this, Nick. It's worth fighting for."

When Callum's eyes met mine again, as kind as his gaze was, it was clear I was thing he was fighting *against* when he fought for the pack.

"What if it's not Misty we're looking for?" Nick asked.

Callum sighed as he drew up a chair across from the couch, and he leaned forward, resting his elbows on his knees. "I don't know everything there is to know about the witches. But I do know there's magic binding Misty, somehow. Why would someone do that to her if she weren't our princess? And she wasn't born in that hospital...her records were obviously forged. All signs point to her."

His gaze lingered on us both in turn. "I'm sorry. I know you want Piper to be...special."

"She is," Nick said firmly.

Callum nodded. "Of course. In her way. All right, Nick. Say good night."

Nick shook his head, his lips tightening rebelliously.

I took his hand in mine. "I don't know anything about this wolf business or fated love or any of that," I said softly, "but what you have here is special already. The four of you. You're a family. Callum's right—it is worth fighting for. I bet he's been fighting for it for a long time."

Callum's eyes widened, and he glanced away, as if I'd accidentally pressed on a tender spot.

"Piper," Nick said.

"I'm already special," I promised him, drawing his hand to my cheek, feeling the warmth of his calloused hand against my skin. "Special enough to have a plan, and my own life going forward. And lucky to have met you."

He shook his head, but he couldn't stop me from saying what else I had to say. "I need you, though. All of you. So I can have my own family—so I can save my little sister—and I can get us out of here. Away from this place, from my father and Eli." The thought of leaving the four of them behind hurt, but it was nothing compared to how badly it would hurt me to stay. "Will you help me with that, Nick? And make your own family, here, because we all need that?"

"You know you have my word," he said reluctantly, "I'll protect you."

"That's not what I'm asking," I said.

"Don't make me promise to send you away," he said. "I want to keep seeing you."

"I know." Tears filled my eyes as I tried to smile. "I want to keep seeing you too. But that's not what's right for either of us. That's not what's right for our families or our future."

"God damn it, Piper," he said.

"Promise me."

His big hands suddenly spanned my jaw, and he kissed me hard. There was so much need in the way his lips devoured mine, and I pressed my palms over his hands, holding him against me, kissing him with just as much desperate need.

But still, when we separated, when there was a breath between us, I stared at him, waiting for my answer.

Finally, he whispered, "I promise."

I nodded, grateful, but it didn't stop the tears that burned my eyes.

Nick suddenly rose from the couch and without looking back, he strode from the room. The door slammed shut behind him.

For long seconds, silence hung in the room. Callum rubbed his hand across his face. Then he finally said, "Thank you, Piper. That was the right thing to do. For you and for him."

"I know," I said dully. "Doesn't make it any easier."

"You're a brave girl," Callum said kindly. "You'll find your way to a happy ending."

"I don't doubt it," I lied. I ran my fingers over the jeweled collar I wore, the one that bound me to Eli. "Now, you made promises to me too. I can't get this off on my own. I need your help."

"Of course," he said. He looked at me strangely. "You know you didn't need to do that for me to help you."

"I know I didn't need to." They were good guys. That was why this was so hard, and why I had to make them choose each other. Not me.

"To put our pack first..." He shook his head. "It was a generous act."

"I'd give anything to have a family like this. To have a *pack*. I wouldn't ask any of you throw that away."

Callum rose and turned his back to me, walking away toward the fireplace. Had I offended him? I stared at him, at the tension in his powerful back and chiseled body.

But after a few long seconds, he said roughly, "Let's get you free, Piper."

20

Josh

I KNEW the tap on the door was Callum, even before I scented him. His knock gave away his personality: heavy-handed and confident.

"Coming." I glanced out the window, at the darkness over the pines, and cursed as I rolled out of bed. Pulling a shirt on hastily over my head, I threw open the door. "You didn't wake me?"

"You're welcome," Callum said, without smiling. "I thought you could use the rest."

"I didn't need rest," I said. "I want to look after Piper."

"You will," he said, and I looked at him uncertainly. I wasn't sure what to make of the promise in his voice. "But how is up to you."

"What are you talking about?" My tone sounded grumpy, but for once, Callum let it pass.

"We need to find Eli Kingston and bring back his blood. Well. Just enough to break the enchantment. We're not going to kill the boy."

He knew how I felt about that, which was probably why he pressed. "Right?"

"Right," I said. "Sure."

"But it's up to you. You can stay here and watch over Piper, or you can go hunt down Eli with me. Either way, you help the girl."

Of course I wanted to stay with Piper. But I was bigger—and meaner—than Nick or Kai. I shoved my hands in my jeans pockets. "You can't hunt him alone. You'll be crossing onto coven land."

"I won't hunt alone," Callum said. "I'm only leaving one of you here to keep the girl company."

"What if Eli comes here looking for her while we're hunting him?" I absently touched my collarbone through my shirt; the thought of a collar like Eli had put on Piper, binding her to him, made my skin burn.

"The witch shouldn't be able to cross our boundaries," Callum said. "If he does, I expect any of you can bring him down."

I didn't like the idea of Kai or Nick facing him alone. I'd only recently learned witches were real, but I knew too well just how evil humans could be, even without dark magic on their side.

If I were here, I'd get a few more hours with Piper. But that was selfish. The most important thing was to make sure she was free.

"We could leave Kai and Nick here," I said. "Just in case."

Callum's eyebrows arched. "I was sure you'd want the time with Piper."

"Of course I do," I said roughly. "But priorities."

"Look at you," he said. "Making the hard choices. You might have the makings of an alpha in the end, after all."

"I won't be an alpha as long as you're alive," I said. "And as much as I might not like being second..."

The thought of losing Callum was jarring. I barely remembered my parents now, or the night we lost everything. Things weren't easy between the two of us, but I did remember one thing.

Callum had saved my life.

"You don't plan to kill me yourself?" Callum finished my sentence drily.

"I've got your back," I said. "You know that."

"I know," he said, but I wasn't sure he did. Callum claimed we'd all gone feral, but he'd been alone for a long time, trying to draw the pack back together. He was single-minded, and he'd turned cold trying to rebuild the family he lost. Sometimes, I didn't think he really believed he'd keep us, in the end.

I wasn't going anywhere, no matter how much he pissed me off, but I didn't have the words to tell him that.

Instead, I said, "Well? You ready to rip an arm off that rapey pretty boy?"

"Josh," he chided. "If we can take him unseen and destroy his memories after, we keep our tactical advantage."

"Fine," I said. "But I hope he fights back."

Callum hid a smile as he turned down the hall.

"What?"

"You might not remember," he said, "but our betas are nothing like humans think when they say *beta*. They're the knights, the warriors of the pack."

"Yeah?"

"You remind me of your dad," he said. "That's all."

That was a lot, but I couldn't ask. I nodded.

"Say goodbye to Piper, if you want," he said. "I'll wake Kai to watch over her for now."

I went down the stairs without answering. In the living room, Piper was asleep again. Her arm was tucked under her cheek, and her lashes rested just above her cheekbones, which were flushed pink from fever. I wanted to touch her—to kiss the round curves of her cheeks, to push her honey-blonde hair back from her face—but it would have been selfish to disturb her sleep. Instead, I gazed at her for a few long seconds.

I wanted to be with her, but the best way I could take care of was to leave. That damned chain was still coiled around her neck. Her throat was white, but her skin looked pink and irritated along the metal outline. My hands knotted into fists.

People mistook me for an idiot, far too often, because I was an upbeat guy. I'd already walked through hell, and I'd decided not to let it turn me into one of the demons. I'd *fought* to find the good in life and to focus on that instead of sliding into cynicism. It was easy to be jaded. It was lazy. Kai didn't like it when I said that, but I was determined to shake my sullen brother out of his habits.

But when someone hurt one of mine...well. The demon was there, I guessed, deep inside. Because I wanted more than anything to hurt Eli.

Piper's eyes fluttered open. I knelt next to the couch. "Sorry," I said softly. "I didn't mean to wake you."

"It's all right. I'd be tossing and turning anyway." Her voice came out husky with sleep, sexy and adorable. "It's nice having someone here when I wake up."

I felt a twinge of guilt for leaving her. Great, there was no winning; apparently, I was going to feel guilty whether I left or stayed.

"Kai's going to watch over you for a while," I said. "I'm going looking for Eli."

She scrambled up onto her elbows. "Josh."

"Yeah?" I wanted to call her something—that *yeah* sounded so harsh without a nickname to soften it—but I wasn't sure she'd like it. And what was she, anyway? A *baby*? A *sweetheart*?

She wasn't supposed to be any of those things to me, and the thought made me feel trapped and furious, all over again, just like that collar around her neck did.

A frown dimpled the space between her clear blue eyes. "What's wrong?"

"Nothing." Finally, I gave into the desire to touch her, smoothing her hair back from her hot forehead with my palm. Her lashes fluttered, as if my touch was pleasant to her, and something stirred in me. Not just lust, or protectiveness. It was something deeper, and unfamiliar, and addictive.

"Be careful," she said. "You shouldn't go...it's dangerous."

"It's not," I assured her. "I'm the most dangerous thing out there tonight. Witches are squishy." I made a squeezing motion with one fist.

Her eyes widened, and she smiled. "That's the most wolfish thing I've heard you say."

"I am what I am," I said.

She chewed on her lower lip, her eyes troubled. I wanted to wrap her in my arms and make her feel better, but she clearly had something she needed to say, so I waited. Finally, she admitted, "I don't know how to deal with this," she touched the necklace, then yanked her fingers away as if it burned, "on my own. But I feel so selfish. I don't want you to get hurt for my sake."

I shook my head. I'd risk my safety for her in a heartbeat. "Don't worry, *I* won't be the one to get hurt."

Her eyes were warm blue pools, like deep ocean water, that I could get lost in. "Eli's dangerous. More dangerous than I thought, and I already thought he was a pretty bad guy..."

"He's a witch," I interrupted. I raised my shirt, showing her the tattoos on my pecs. "Yes, he's dangerous. But I'm warded to block his magic."

She leaned forward, her eyes intent, and lifted her fingertips as if to touch my ink. My abs contracted, my body practically vibrating with desire, but her fingertips hovered an inch away from my pecs and then fell. "But...then how..."

"The power of wards was something Callum discovered *after* most of our family was murdered." A bitter note crept into my voice, and I shook my head, clearing it away. Packs lived in isolation, avoiding other packs. It was dangerous. If the packs shared information, if they weren't *stupid,* my parents might still be alive.

"Let me do what I'm going to do," I went on, more softly. "You and I might not be fated to love each other, Piper. But I can tell you, I'll always be your friend. I'll always have your back."

She glanced away, her eyes suddenly liquid blue. "Let me help, somehow..."

"You can help by staying here and recovering while I chase down that cowardly witch," I said firmly. And then, a bit more tentatively, I added, "And a kiss for good luck wouldn't hurt."

Her eyes met mine and widened. Her face shifted, as if I'd just chased away the sadness—for the moment, anyway—and she closed the distance between us, pressing her lips against mine.

Whenever she was close to me, my heart raced, my blood heated, and some primitive inner part of my growled *mine*. I couldn't help wrapping my arms around her hard, kissing her back as fiercely as I felt. She grinned against my lips, and then the smile fell away. Whatever she'd found funny was lost as we traded kisses. Her hands caressed my abs, pressing against my waist.

She grabbed my belt, pulling me toward her as she fell back into the pillows. Her fingers against my jeans, against my thigh, made me harden. I braced myself with an arm on the couch, holding my weight away from her. As her lips sought mine, I broke away, pressing kisses to her neck, tracing my way down to her throat. She moaned, a ragged, eager sound. Her bare foot traced up my calf, as if she was about to pin my legs to hers.

"Well?" Callum said from the doorway, his voice harsh and impatient.

I pulled away from her in a hurry. "Knocking, Callum. It's a thing. And you say *we* went feral."

"Feral's not about human manners, boy. It's about loyalty to the pack."

"I'm loyal," I promised, but my gaze was still on Piper's. Those gorgeous, liquid-blue eyes stared back into mine, then crinkled at the corners, as if she heard my promise to her.

I leaned forward, kissing her one more time. Her lips were soft and sweet.

"I'll be back to break that enchantment before you know it," I told her, standing from the couch.

"Are you sure this is what we need to do?" she asked. "There isn't another way? Something safer?"

"Nah," I told her. "There's not a lot of *something safe* in the world of witches and wolves."

"We'll get that curse broken and help you and Maddie set up somewhere far away from here, if that's what you want," Callum said firmly. "Somewhere you'll never have to think about witches or wolves ever again."

A rueful smile twisted her pretty lips. "I have a funny feeling I'll keep thinking about wolves."

Something stabbed in my chest at the thought. Jesus, was she going to miss me as much as I'd miss her?

There was no way this was right.

I'd fight fate too, if it came down to it. There was no way some pack lore was stronger than my own instincts. They'd kept me alive so far.

But for now, I had to protect her.

Callum grunted in response to her words. Then he jerked his head toward the door. "Let's go. We're burning night."

I pulled a face behind his back—and the smile she gave me in response warmed my chest—then followed.

By the time we were crossing the backyard, we were stripping. I stopped under the moonlight at the edge of the trees to roll my clothes into a ball with my shoes inside. Usually, if I knew I'd have to shift back, I only carried my jeans—the more shit I had to carry in my jaws, the harder it was to move and the rougher it was on my wardrobe—but tonight, I might just have to stroll into the party and drag Eli Kingston out by his hair. That was worth sinking my teeth into flannel.

"Ready?" Callum asked as I tied the last knot.

I dropped the bundle into the grass in answer. "Let's do this."

The change never came easy. I heard my voice groan, and then change into an animal sound, the desperate sound of a wolf in pain. As my muscles shifted, they became charged with energy and restlessness.

The big white head of the alpha wolf shoved into my side, checking in on me, and I made a soft sound in response. Still fully human, and yet wolf at the same time. Callum's eyes glittered as he checked me over, making sure I was okay, then he turned and ran into the woods. I was glad to run, to let my powerful muscles loose and feel alive as I raced through the forest.

We reached the edge of the lake and ran through the soft mud of the bank as a cool rain began to fall. Then the lights of the lake house were in front of us, visible through the lattice of branches at the edge of the lake. I dropped my bundle and began the change.

A few minutes later, I cursed as I rubbed my sore shoulders. The lingering ache in my joints was the worst part of the change.

"You going to put on your pants?" Callum asked drily. He was already dressed, and he crossed barefoot to the edge of the lake. He dipped his hand slowly into the black water, careful not to make a sound as he glanced toward the house, to slap the water into his face. He shook his head as he stood. But that was the only sign he showed of having a tough time with the change.

"I haven't had as much practice as you, sorry." I'd started the transformation a few years before, when I still lived with my adoptive parents. I'd been convinced that the wolves and witches that haunted my dreams were nothing but childhood nightmares. Then I found myself waking up naked and terrified in the forest, a few shreds of my clothes still clinging around my wrists and legs, with the taste of blood in my mouth and a blinding headache.

Eli Kingston was going to think he'd gotten blackout drunk in the morning, but he had no idea what a transformation hangover was like.

"Putting on pants?"

"You know what I mean." I pulled on my shirt and shoved my feet into my shoes, then moved next to him in the brush. "You see the loser?"

He nodded, his nostrils flaring. I followed his gaze to the house. A bunch of loudmouth guys congregated on the deck overlooking the water, smoking cigars and chatting. Eli seemed to be among them. A couple stumbled out of the house and into their car, which was parked at the front of the house. "I think it's clearing out. Not a lot of people anymore, and the music's turned down."

"Maybe he'll leave soon and we can get him on the way."

"I thought you wanted to go in there and kick his ass," Callum said.

"I do." He didn't need to rub my nose in the fact I was following *his* goddamn plan, whether I liked it or not.

The silence stretched between us as we watched the house. It lasted long enough for me to wonder if he meant it that way, or if I was just reading the worst in him.

It would help if Callum ever just *talked*. He mostly gave orders. Who knew what the hell went on in his head?

"I thought the alpha and the beta usually had a mutual respect," I said. Was it just because I was younger than he was?

He didn't look away from the house, but his eyebrows arched. "I do respect you, Josh."

Sure.

"Do I trust you where your heart's involved?" he went on. "Well. Let's not get carried away."

Oh, there was the usual barb.

"It's not my heart," I said. "It's my instinct. Shouldn't a wolf follow his instincts?"

"That girl means well," he said. "But she's poison to our pack."

I shook my head. "And yet. You want to help her?"

"Because she *does* mean well, and she's an innocent, I want to help her by moving her far from here," he said bluntly. "I don't know why you fixed on her, but we mate for life, and you already have a mate. And I'm done discussing it."

That was the longest speech I'd heard Callum give in a long time, and I wasn't going to make things better by testing him now.

My lips tightened, holding back anything else I might say.

"I promised your father I'd look after you," Callum said. "And I've fucked it all up, but I'm not going to stop trying."

His face in profile was expressionless, but I didn't think he felt nothing when he said it.

"Shouldn't you be keeping an eye on Eli?" he said gruffly.

My gaze snapped back to the deck. "He doesn't seem like he's going anywhere in a hurry."

"All right," Callum said. "Go get him."

"You sure?"

"Don't give away that you know anything about the spell," Callum said. "Just find an excuse to kick his ass. Do your best to chase him toward the woods—I'll take care of it if you get him close."

I nodded.

One corner of Callum's mouth curled up, and he clapped me on the shoulder. "You should see the look on your face. Like it's Christmas."

"You don't need to buy me a present this year," I said, pushing my sleeves up my forearms.

There was just something magic about kicking the ass of the man who hurt your girl.

Even if no one else thought she could ever be yours.

I skirted the edge of the woods so I could emerge, unseen, into the driveway and the tire-pitted front yard. After crossing the porch, I accidentally slammed open the door to the lake house. Maybe I had a little too much enthusiasm right now.

The living room was empty now, the lights turned down low, although there were beer bottles and red cups everywhere. Looking through to the end of the house, I could see the patio doors standing open to the deck. The air stank of human sweat and lust, and sour beer and sickly-sweet punch. My nostrils flared.

"Who's there?" someone called from the deck. "You bring Jenny back?"

There was scattered laughter from the seven guys still on the deck. I'd counted before I came in.

"Not Jenny," I called back. The door in front of me was half open, so I pushed it the rest of the way open and stepped out onto the deck.

Eli's eyes narrowed. "I'm glad you're here."

"Oh, I'm so glad to be here."

He almost tripped as he headed toward me, his movement jerky—the combination of rage and drunk was not his friend—and jabbed his finger in my chest. "You think you're such hot shit. But you're not—"

I wasn't getting into a verbal sparring match with him. I smiled back at him, glancing at the rest of the guys. They were standing back for now, watching this situation escalate, puffing on their cigars and leaning against the railing. For right now, I was the entertainment.

I grabbed Eli's throat and shoved him across the deck. Someone swore and someone dove out of my way, and by the time anyone even though about coming after me, Eli clawed at my shoulders as his back slammed into the deck railing.

Now there was someone at my back, but I was already ducking low, so they hit the railing above me, just before I grabbed Eli around the legs and launched myself up.

He flipped over the railing and screamed just before he plummeted...all six feet to the gravel.

I elbowed the guy who'd come after me out of my way and vaulted the railing after him, landing lightly on my feet.

Eli struck me as a guy who liked a fight, but maybe I'd misjudged him. He was groaning as he got to his feet, and he glowered at me. "What the hell are you doing?"

"What did you do to Piper?" I asked. "She was scared of you."

"Is this really what this is about?" He rubbed his shoulder. "You came storming in here because that little whore cried to you?"

"You should really try to throw a punch. I'm going to feel guilty about this otherwise."

"I'm going to kill you," Eli promised me. "No matter what happens tonight. You'd better watch your back."

"Are you going to throw that punch?" I looked up at the guys crowding the railing, currently not helping their friend, and raised my hands in an exaggerated gesture of frustration. "Guess your buddy's a coward. Who didn't see that coming?"

He finally launched himself at me, trying to tackle me around the waist. I twisted to one side, catching his ankle with mine, and knocked him down. I glanced toward the woods as he fell, knowing Callum was out there. I hadn't expected it to be difficult to get Eli to fight me. What the hell was wrong with this kid?

He threw himself into my legs, and I came down on top of him, punching him across the face. I hit him a second time, then shoved him away from me, and he rolled across the grass.

He sprang to his feet and sprinted toward the front of the house, where the cars were parked. I slammed into his side, knocking him off balance, and shoved him toward the woods. There was a hollering on the deck—his friends had finally decided to help him—and I glanced behind me to see the coast clear for a second as his friends piled through the house.

"Now," I called as I shoved Eli into the shadows.

Eli turned his head to look back at me, rage and helplessness in his eyes, just before Callum clapped the wet towel in his hand over Eli's mouth and nose. I blinked hard as my own eyes began to sting from the chemical scent. Eli struggled, making a desperate sound, before he lurched to the ground.

"Those assholes are going to help us out and they don't even know it," Callum said. He threw Eli over his shoulders easily, and the two of us ran through the woods, ducking under branches and twisting through the brush. Even in human form, it wasn't hard to outrun them—our vision was sharper in the night and we were faster than any true human.

It bought us the time for Callum to dump Eli between two fallen oak trees. He unzipped his backpack and quickly rolled up the sleeve of Eli's fleece, tapping the crook of his elbow to fatten the vein. Then he slid a needle in quickly, filling a syringe with blood.

As soon as he had tucked the syringes carefully into a hard shell case, he slid another needle, loaded with yellow fluid, into that same vein. "There. He won't remember the last hour."

That was a pity. "I hope someone tells him what a coward he was."

"Something to look forward to at school on Monday," Callum said, shaking his head as he zipped his backpack up. "Sometimes I forget what a boy you still are. All right, those fools don't seem as close on our heels as I expected. We'll have to drag him back."

I sighed, but grabbed Eli's wrist, carefully pulling his sleeve back down to hide the trickle of blood. Then I put my shoulder into his stomach and lifted him up. His weight settled heavily on my shoulders and neck, and holding him so close to me made me bristle with irritation.

Callum started to say something—he'd planned to carry him, I'd bet—but stopped. He nodded his thanks, then yanked off his shirt. "I'll turn, it'll make it easier to scent them. When I stop, drop him."

"Can't wait."

When Callum transformed, I looked away. It seemed rude to watch; it was such a bloody, intimate, painful thing. He picked up the backpack with his teeth, and the big wolf streaked off ahead of me.

We dumped Eli where his friends would find him—so close we could hear their voices as they stumbled drunkenly through the woods—and then ran back to the house.

Time to free Piper. From all of us, if that was what she chose.

21

P*iper*

"I can't sleep," I told Kai as I sat up. "Shouldn't they be back yet? What if they got caught?"

"They're fine," Kai said.

There was faint noise in the hall, and my head swiveled toward it as my heart leapt. *Josh?*

Kai stared at me, as if he weren't at all worried about Callum and Josh. "Did you hear that?"

"Is that them?" I asked.

He snapped his fingers. "Focus, Piper. Did you hear that?"

I stared back at him. "Yes…"

The door opened, and Josh burst in. Callum followed, a backpack thrown over one shoulder.

"You're okay," Josh said, his eyes meeting mine, relief written across his face.

"You sound surprised when I've done nothing but sleep, and

you've been out there running around attacking…wizards." It still felt ridiculous to use that word.

"Kai, do you have everything I asked you to gather?" Callum asked, but Kai was already bringing a bowl from the table in the corner. Callum shoved the coffee table out of the way, and Josh rolled up the carpet to reveal a square of plain, dark hardwood.

Kai knelt with the bowl. Callum quickly ran through its contents, checking that everything was there. Then he struck a match and touched it to the contents. The fire caught quickly. The herbs in the bowl turned black and wilted, and little white flames licked upward. A strange, sharp herbal scent filled the air.

"You use magic too," I said. "What makes you different than the wizards?"

"We don't say wizards," Josh said. "Because being a *wizard* sounds fun. Magic isn't fun. It's always bound in blood. Yours or someone else's."

Callum unscrewed a syringe of blood and poured it onto the flames, dousing them, as he muttered in Latin.

"We only use defensive magic," Josh explained. "Or we'll undo a spell. No one needs to have that kind of power in this world."

Callum finished his spell and, as he reached his hand into sift through the ash, he explained, "Magic itself isn't bad. But the people who seek out that kind of power, who are willing to bleed themselves at first—well, they tend to end up wanting to bleed other people, sooner or later. Power is corrupting."

"But the magic of being a werewolf is different?" I was so curious to understand their world, even if I wasn't supposed to be a part of it.

"It's not magic," Callum said impatiently. "It's who we are. Lie down."

I wriggled onto the pillow on the couch, and he leaned over me. He broke the ashes apart in his fist, sprinkling them down on my throat as he incanted some words in Latin. My eyes drifted shut, listening to him, waiting for magic to take me over. His voice was all warm honey, sexy and masculine, when his words weren't so sharp. It was nice to listen to.

His fingers touched the necklace, drawing it away from my skin. Pain lanced through my throat, so intense it stole my breath. I grabbed his hand to keep him from touching it again as I scrambled up. I took deep frantic breaths, feeling as if I couldn't fill my lungs again.

"It didn't work," Kai said. "Do you have more blood?"

"It's not the spell that went wrong," Callum said. "I know I did that right, I've done it before."

"Then what's the problem?" Kai demanded.

Callum flashed him a warning look. "It's got to be the blood. Someone else put that curse together for Eli."

Josh strode across the room, raking a hand through his hair. "Who the hell would support his obsession with Piper? Who would go that far?"

"His dad is pretty fond of him," I said. The words came out raspy, but at least I could talk. "If they're both witches. Or maybe they paid someone. Oh…is that how they came to be so powerful in this town?"

Callum rubbed my thigh comfortingly. I didn't give away that I noticed, because I didn't think he even realized—he'd moved to take care of me when agony raced through my throat, and his hand had still been on my thigh when the pain eased.

"I'd imagine," Callum said. He seemed to realize what he was doing, and he suddenly stood from the couch, tucking his hands inside his pockets. He flashed me a quick, tight smile. "Well, don't worry, Piper. We'll just have to do some detective work."

I nodded, but I had to wonder how far he would go to help me. Just then, my purse vibrated from the chair next to the fire. I stood, then swayed on my feet, my vision fading black around the edges. When the humming in my ears dimmed and my head cleared, the guys were crowded around me.

They were hovering. There was no other word for it.

"My purse," I said, gesturing to Kai, who was closest to it, since I was framed in by their protective bodies. "I'm fine, guys."

Kai picked up my purse, scooping it up with two hands and holding it from the bottom as if it was some kind of sacred relic. He offered it to me, and I grabbed the strap as I sat heavily again on the couch. I really didn't feel quite right, even now.

"What exactly does this necklace to do me?" I asked. "Since apparently I'm going to spend a little longer with it?"

My voice came out much calmer than I felt. Having this chain around my neck made me feel frantic, like I had to escape it.

I unzipped my purse and rooted through it for my cell phone, even though I'd already missed the call while I tried not to pass out.

"It will make it difficult for you to disobey the blood that marked the necklace," Callum said. "You will feel compelled to do whatever the magician says."

The thought of Eli controlling me made me feel sick to my stomach, as if the world were an even darker, dirtier place than I ever realized. I could imagine the two of us in school, his arm over my shoulders. *I want to own you.* A shiver ran up my spine, and Josh's eyes sharpened. He brushed the back of my fingers with his hand, and I twined my fingers in his, taking strength from his touch.

Josh suggested, "Maybe it was Eli's father or some other blood relative, because then there's a possibility the necklace's powers would extend to him..."

"True," Callum said. "We'll definitely look at his family first."

"Maybe there's someone else who wanted to enchant Piper," Kai said. "Eli's a creep, sure. But we have to look at all the options."

"You're right. Do you have any other enemies, Piper?" Callum asked.

The only enemy I could think of was my father. But it seemed so ridiculous to imagine him as a witch. "How many witches do you think there are in this town?"

"Quite a few," Callum said. "But whoever is behind the enchantment, we can keep you safe until we figure it out."

His protectiveness, no matter how he felt about me, still warmed my chest.

"So you want Piper to stay?" Josh asked casually.

"I want Piper safe," Callum said, choosing his words carefully. "If that means she stays... for now... then she stays."

The missed call was from Maddie. I started to replay her message and lifted the phone to my ear.

"Something's been bothering me," Kai said. "I know all evidence points to Misty."

"That's right," Callum said.

"But I'm not convinced Piper is—"

As much as I wanted to know what Kai thought I was—and wasn't—their voices were lost the second I heard Maddie draw a strangled breath.

There was a long pause, and then she said, in a tear-filled voice, "Piper. Are you coming home? Where are you?"

My chest tightened. Oh my god. My little sister, who always worried she was going to be abandoned. I hadn't come home last night. She must feel so frightened and alone.

"I hope you're coming home soon," she whispered, and then there was a long pause before she said, "Goodbye." Then she hung up.

"I've got to get home," I said, throwing my purse into my bag. "Thank you, guys, so much for everything, but I have to go."

"You can't leave," Callum said firmly.

"My sister is scared and alone," I said. "I have to go home. In the long run, I always had to go home eventually."

"Not with that collar," Callum said. "That chain around your neck isn't just for show. Someone will want to use it."

"I won't leave the house," I couldn't help absently running my fingertips over the damned necklace, even though just touching it sent warning tingles of pain seeping into my skin, like fresh bruises. "Believe me, I'm not excited about it either."

"It's not safe," Josh said. Unlike Callum's commanding tone, his was gentle, but laced with urgency. "Piper, please. If you need to see your sister, we can go get her."

They meant well, but I shook my head. "And you *kidnap* her? She'd be terrified. I'm trying to make things better, not worse. But I'll stay in touch with you guys. I won't leave the house without you."

Kai gazed at me like I was a puzzle he was trying to figure out. He was silent, and I wondered why.

With his arms crossed, Callum drummed his fingers against his bicep. He was weighing the options, and I found myself waiting for his decision, just like Josh and Kai.

Of course, if he said *no*, I was going anyway. I hated to imagine what might happen if I tried to leave the house against his wishes, so hopefully he was swayed by my argument.

I wasn't leaving my father's control just to follow another man's orders.

Callum nodded, a quick, curt jerk of his head. "I don't like it. But if that's what you believe you must do."

"It is."

"Then I'll drive you home," Josh said. His mouth tightened, as if he hated being separated from me in this situation.

"No," Callum said sharply. "You shouldn't be out there right now. There may be people looking for you."

"What do you mean, people looking for him?" I eyed Callum, then Josh. "Are you in danger? Because you tried to help me?"

"He'll be fine," Callum said. "This will all blow over soon. We just can't be sure that Eli and his friends, or his father's lackeys—whether they're witches or the local police—won't want revenge for Josh kicking Eli's ass."

I knit my arms over my chest. Great. Another weight to carry. I'd ruined Blissford for Josh.

"They won't be in power long," Callum promised, as if he could read me. "Once we've formed our full pack, we'll be strong enough to knock any evil out of Blissford. For now, we'll lie low. Kai and Nick can take you home."

"Okay. Thank you." Unless I wanted to walk ten miles home, I had no choice but to accept their help, in this and in so much more. It was a strange feeling for me. I'd gotten used to depending only on myself.

"I'll get Nick," Kai said, disappearing from the room on near-silent feet. They all moved so quietly.

"Let me walk you to the car." Josh slung my purse over his shoulder and held his hand out to me to steady me as I stood.

I rested my hand in his and let him help me up, although I

couldn't help the smile that came to my lips at the sight of big, rough-hewn, athletic Josh with a dainty purse slung over his shoulder. It was just like him to be completely unselfconscious. As funny as I found the scene, I admired his steadfast, quiet self-confidence.

He watched over me carefully as we headed toward the door to the study. Then he seemed to relax, once he was sure I'd found my feet.

"Goodbye for now, Piper," Callum said. "You can always call. We'll be here when you need us."

When, not *if*.

"Wouldn't it be easier for you if I just disappeared?" I asked over my shoulder. I'd meant the words to come out teasing, light-hearted.

They didn't.

Callum's gaze met mine, his face cool and dispassionate as ever, his eyes unreadable. "No."

Well, that was... succinct. Certainly made a girl feel better about her life.

Josh pushed open the door, and the two of us stepped into the two-story foyer. Dawn had just broken, gold streaking the sky just above the pines but not yet shattering the blue-black night above. Had Maddie been up all night, waiting for me? My heart twisted at the thought. If I called her back, and my dad overheard, I'd be in so much trouble. Best to see if I could slip inside before he woke up. I'd climb into bed with Maddie, if she wasn't still awake staring at the ceiling, and tuck her head under my chin.

He walked with me across the yard, and my muscles tensed as cold seeped in. When he opened the car door for me, I paused. This close, my eyes were level with his collar bones, and I breathed in the menthol scent of his aftershave. He was so much taller than me, and yet he never seemed intimidating. I looked up and found him gazing down at me, a frown crinkling his forehead above his ocean blue eyes.

There didn't seem to be anything left to say. They'd tried so hard to help me, and I could tell it hurt Josh to see me leave. I wanted to tell him I'd be fine, but I couldn't make the words form on my lips. I wasn't sure that was true. And when he gazed at me, his kissable lips pursed about his hard-edged jaw, it seemed impossible to lie to him.

I caught his shoulders with my hands and stretched on my tiptoes to kiss him goodbye. Since words failed me, a kiss seemed like the best way to leave things.

He caught me around the waist, his hand in the small of my back, and his lips pressed against mine, sweet and sure. As our kisses turned more intense, his arm around me tightened. My lips tingled forth, and then those pleasant tingles seemed to sweep through my body, inflaming my desire for him. His fingers tangled in my hair, tugging on my scalp, and the pleasant tingles turned to waves of hot, desperate desire.

He broke away, breathing hard. I touched my aching lips. What the hell was that? He was a gorgeous, kind, funny guy—it made sense I would have a crush on him. But no matter how wonderful he was, the depth of my feelings after we'd only known each other a few days seemed like madness.

"Don't give up," he said, his hands going to my hips, holding me there. "We'll figure everything out. Together."

I wasn't sure what he meant I shouldn't give up on—destroying the necklace, or my future, or our affection for each other? "I don't give up. That's not who I am."

I wanted to believe I could force a happy ending, no matter how dark the skies still were overhead.

He brushed his lips quickly, sweetly, over my cheek, then pulled the door open fully, ushering me in. From the corner of my eye, I caught sight of Nick and Kai, crossing the yard toward us, and I wondered if they'd been waiting, giving us time to say goodbye.

I slipped into the seat, and Josh closed the door firmly behind me. As he stepped back, he looked at me through the window. The strangest feeling coursed through me. *I'm seeing him for the last time.*

It was a ridiculous thought, but maybe Josh saw its shadow cross my face, because he looked at me as if he wanted to pull me back out of the car and wrap me in his arms. But I had to go home, so I did my best to smile and raised my hand in a wave. He lifted his hand as well, and then the doors were opening, and Kai slid into the driver's seat and Nick got in in behind me.

"Morning," Nick said, and I twisted in my seat to greet him. When I glanced back out the window, Josh was climbing the stairs to the front porch. The breeze ruffled his dark blond hair, and his flannel shirt hugged his leanly muscled frame.

Kai started the car, then puffed into his hands before he turned the wheel, and I turned to watch the tree branches interwoven above the long driveway. Going home made me restless and anxious, and I wanted to stay here so badly, but I had to take care of my little sister.

It was hard to believe that just a few days ago, I'd driven Kai home with…Nick the wolf in the backseat. "I can't wait to critique your driving."

"I'll do my best not to cry," he deadpanned.

"You are such a jerk," I said, shaking my head, but I didn't really mind. Kai was Kai. He was all hard edges, but at his core, he was full of sweet kisses and gentle nicknames.

We made small talk as they drove me home, but I didn't have my heart in the conversation, and it didn't seem like they did either. With every mile the car sped down the road, more dread filled my stomach. I tucked my hair behind my ears, full of nervous energy. My father usually slept late on the weekends. Hopefully he wouldn't notice I'd been gone all night.

Nick and Kai fell quiet as we neared home.

"Just stop on the street." I didn't want them to pull in the driveway, since that would make it more likely my father would hear.

"Do you want us to wait and make sure you get in okay?" Nick asked.

"If you wait, I won't be okay," I said lightly, imagining how my father would react to me coming home with a few boys—er, men?—I didn't know.

My light tone didn't go over, because Kai's lips tightened. "All right." He threw a meaningful look over his shoulder at Nick, which I didn't miss.

"Go home," I said firmly.

"Of course," Nick said easily. He rested his big hand on my shoulder and squeezed gently.

Getting out of the car and leaving them behind me, to walk up that long driveway to the big, foreboding house, felt like leaving the sunshine behind to walk into a blizzard.

22

When I let myself into the house, everything was quiet and still. I carried my purse stiffly across the entryway to the stairs, listening for any sound. Maybe Maddie had fallen asleep after her teary message. When she woke up, I'd be there and everything would be okay.

"Good morning, Piper," my father said acerbically from the doorway to the kitchen.

God damn it. I stopped with my foot on the first stair and faced him. "Good morning, Dad."

"When I said you could choose your own curfew, I thought the same boy who took you out would bring you home." His voice was deadly quiet. "Instead, Eli's father says he was attacked last night...by a boy you seem to have taken a shine to. A boy who's all bad news."

"Eli wasn't very nice to me last night," I said, in the understatement of the century. But I couldn't tell my father about the magic. He wouldn't believe me.

But if he did, that would be even worse. The last thing my father needed was to add to his power.

"You've been nothing but trouble since the day you were born," he said. "It was a terrible storm that night. The Heavens rattling, lightning striking the trees around the house. It was like God himself was furious about your entry into the universe."

Well, that was a nice bedtime story. It was one I'd heard before. My father loved to talk about how I'd always been a pain in the ass.

"Maybe God was just excited about what an awesome little person He'd just sent off into the world," I said, my mouth moving faster than my brain. I'd thought it before, but I didn't mean to say it. Every once in a while, my love of a good quip overwhelmed my self-preservation instincts. I flashed a smile at my father, hoping to soften my words and sound like I wasn't arguing with him. "It sounds like it was quite the birthday party to me."

Something dark flashed in his eyes, like a memory had just occurred to him. "Oh, it was. It's too bad you don't remember."

"That childhood amnesia." I found the phenomenon fascinating; little children were supposed to remember their births and toddler years, then forget them before they were old enough to tell us much about what they'd seen. I wished I remembered any of my early days; I didn't have any memories of a mother who loved me.

My father's gaze sharpened, fixed on my neck. I'd tucked the necklace into my shirt, and now I fought the impulse to reach up and touch my collar, to make sure it was still hidden.

"Who gave you that, Piper?" he asked.

He was going to be even more furious I'd disrespected his friend's son after Eli had given me a gift. Lying wouldn't help me now, though. "Eli."

He was at my side in two quick strides, and he grabbed my necklace with his fingers, trying to wrench it away. I cried out as pain raced through my body, my vision darkening around the edges. My knees buckled, and I collapsed to the cold tiles.

"What did you do?" he ground through gritted teeth.

Then he grabbed the necklace in his fist and yanked me across the floor. I fought to pry his fingers away. I kicked out, trying to get a purchase with my heels on the slick floor, but I couldn't stop him. He dragged me relentlessly through the house to the garage as the metal cut into my throat.

It was only when he'd gotten the trunk open that he released his grip on my necklace. Before I could gather my wits, he bent and grabbed me around the legs, tossing me easily into the back of the car.

His furious eyes met mine as I reached up for the hatch, trying to stop him from closing me in.

"Please don't," I said, my voice coming out broken and raspy; I coughed, still choking from the way he'd dragged me. "Please."

There had to be some part of him that loved me, or that had loved me once. I had to reach that part of him.

He didn't say anything. He just slammed the trunk shut.

Suddenly I was all alone in the black fabric interior. I drew a panicked breath. *Calm down, Piper. You need to get ready to fight back. Don't wimp out now.*

Well, maybe I could take a minute or two to panic.

I searched frantically across the rough black fabric. I'd been carrying my purse. Had I dropped it in the struggle? If I had my phone, I'd have a chance. Or where was the release—there was a release on the inside of every trunk, but I didn't know where it was. I searched frantically until I found a wire loop to one side of the hatch, and I yanked on it desperately. Nothing happened.

My father might have always planned for things to end up like this.

I hadn't found his emergency kit either. If I could find scissors, or a flare, or something I could use for a weapon...but it seemed as though he had stripped everything out of the trunk. Tears blurred my eyes in my frustration, but I blinked them away. *Think, Piper.*

The car shook, the rumble of road noise loud as if we were traveling over gravel, and the cold seeped into my muscles, making them even more sore and tense. The prolonged pain from the necklace had left every muscle aching.

I was going to have to be smart. Was my father bringing me out into the woods to kill me, or did he have another plan?

The car slowed. I curled up on my side, drawing my knees up to protect my organs. I wanted to be ready to launch myself out of the car, but I wasn't sure I had the strength in my muscles now.

When the car stopped, I fought a sharp rise of bile. I was terrified, and the adrenaline flooding my body wasn't helping when I couldn't move. The minutes ticked by, and I was left alone.

The trunk popped open. My father looked down at me, a dark metal gun in his hand. The barrel took all my attention. It gaped wide, staring at me, full of the promise of death.

"Get out," my father said impatiently. "I'm not going to hurt you, Piper. I just didn't want your sister to see you like this. And I know you—I don't want any of your antics."

For Maddie to see me like this? Like *what*? Still, he stepped back from the car, gesturing with the gun.

I swiveled my legs over the back of the hatch and eased myself out, testing my unsteady legs. As soon as I was out, my father grabbed the necklace at the back of my neck, inadvertently ripping out the strands of my hair in his way. I groaned, and then the pain lanced through my neck, radiating through my body. My knees weakened again.

"It hurts." My voice came out as a whimper.

He jerked me close to him, so my ear was close to his mouth, before he said, "Oh, I know."

"What's going on?" I asked. "Dad? Where are we going?"

"I'm not going to hurt you," he said, proving—once again—that he and I had very different definitions of *hurt*.

I was pretty sure he meant he wasn't going to kill me, at least not yet, which was a pretty low bar to set on parenting.

"You're lucky Maddie's useless to me still," he said, dragging me toward a small hunting cabin in front of us.

Hearing my sister's name on his lips gave me a spike of energy, and I reached back to grab his hand. He wrenched harder on the necklace, which gouged deep into my throat, cutting off my airway. I gagged as pain spiked through my throat, worse than before. When I stumbled, my father just dragged me with him, up the stairs that loomed large in my vision, across the porch.

He pushed open the door and I had the blurriest sense of the room around us—a fireplace, a kitchen counter, a bed in the corner—before I saw the open trap door, the rug rolled back haphazardly next to it.

"Your choice if you climb down the ladder or fall down," my father said, his voice calm.

"I'll go," I said, desperate to get his hand off me for a minute.

"I don't want to shoot you, Piper, but I will," he said, and I didn't doubt him. "You'll survive a leg wound, but it will make you quite uncomfortable."

"I'll go down," I said.

"Good." He released me. The barrel of the gun gazed at me again. "Good girl. Go."

Reluctantly, I looked down into the dim light of the room below, then stepped onto the first rung of the ladder. I descended on unsteady legs, my hands shaking so badly on the rungs I feared I'd slip and fall.

At the bottom, I stepped onto a cold earth floor. In one corner of the room was a cage, and across from it was a table and a chair. Bare bulbs illuminated the rough plywood walls. I looked up at him in panic. "How long have you been planning this?"

"Since before you were born," he said. "Go into the cage and close the door. Bang the door shut. I want to hear it."

I didn't see any escape, so reluctantly, I went into the cage. Inside was a mattress on the floor, a blanket and pillow folded at the foot of the bed, and a bucket. There was a package of plastic water bottles and a box of granola bars, too. The metal ceiling brushed against the top of my head as I turned and reluctantly took the metal door in my hand, swinging it shut. It clanged hard.

He wouldn't have gone through all this to kill me. Not yet. *Survive and fight another day.*

Satisfied, he holstered the gun and climbed down the ladder himself. When he reached the bottom and turned to face me, his gaze fell on the necklace again, and his eyes blazed with anger.

"Who put the necklace on you?" he asked, his voice full of controlled fury.

"Eli," I said.

"That boy doesn't have the kind of magic to work that spell alone," he muttered.

"He said he didn't want to date me...he wanted to own me."

He shushed me impatiently, holding a finger to his lips as he paced across the room. Finally, he stopped, crossing his arms. "It would be nice if this were nothing but an overindulgent father giving his son the girl he wants."

I don't know that I'd call it *nice,* personally.

"But I think Alan Kingston's finally moved against me," he said. "He wants control of you for himself."

"Dad," I said. "Please tell me what's going on."

A cold smile twisted his lips. "You can stop calling me Dad. It's always been a farce—and from the way you've acted since you were a child, you've always felt it too."

"I'm not your daughter?"

"But you were my most prized possession. At least until I found Maddie. But she hasn't yet come into her powers." He shook his head. "Saves your life, girl. I've got to get that collar off you and keep you breathing until Maddie's old enough to be useful. But that doesn't mean you need to see sunlight."

His words chilled me. As much as I needed answers, I found my fingers curling around the cold, hard bars. "Please. Come on, you raised me. You must have felt something—"

"Oh, I felt something," he said. "The frustration of having to look at your sullen face every day has been outweighed by the power coursing through my veins."

"Please just tell me what's going on," I pleaded. The more I understood, the better my chances of finding a way out.

"You're not human," he said. "You're a werewolf. The spark of magic inside you—the princess of the pack—burns bright and fierce enough to power a whole coven."

Almost to himself, he added, "But someone always has to get

greedy. Alan must have seen a chance to take you for his own and used Eli to put that chain around your neck. Stupid girl."

"Well, maybe you could have filled me in earlier." Tension twisted my stomach, my emotions roiling so much I could barely understand what I felt. I was terrified, but also... I was the pack princess? The one Callum and the boys searched for? But Callum was so convinced it was Misty...

He snorted. "If you knew I murdered your parents and stole you from your pack, I'm sure that would have made you less rebellious, hm?"

What did he know about the guys? The thought made ice crystals unfurl inside my stomach. "Why didn't my pack ever come looking for me?"

"They're all dead." He flashed me a tight, cruel smile. "You're no princess now. But your powers can still be useful to us."

"If I'm a werewolf," I stumbled over the word, which still felt strange to use, "How come I've never changed?"

"Your powers are drained in our regular rituals." He made finger quotes. "Poker night."

"You give me pizza and take away the thing that makes me..."

"Special?" he filled in. "You aren't special, Piper. You're just useful."

"Wait. If you killed everyone in my pack, how did you get Maddie?"

"She's another pack's princess," he said. "She only came to us four years ago."

"I remember Maddie being born," I said. I remembered all those years when she was little and growing up."

"You think you do." His voice was gleeful. "Your own magic powered the coven to rewrite your memory."

"Wait. Who else is in the coven? Eli's father. Is Eli...?" When I found Callum again, he would want to know who was in the coven, who'd destroyed our pack. *Our pack.*

I had to survive, because I'd go home to Josh and Nick and Kai.

"He's too young and stupid," my father said, "although apparently

Alan told him more than he should have, while he was plotting to steal you from me. I'm going to kill him. I'm going to kill them both."

"What happens to me?" I asked.

"You rot here," he said. He turned to the ladder, then paused. "I almost forgot."

He dragged the table toward me, stopping it just out of reach, and stepped back to gauge the distance. Then he set up a battery powered baby monitor.

"I don't want to leave you without entertainment," he said. "One videotape deserves another, don't you think, Piper?"

He stepped away, revealing a grainy color image of my sister's room. She was still in bed, one arm tossed across her face, blocking out the sunlight. She looked so little, and my heart twisted, seeing her there.

"Enjoy the movie," he said.

When he left, he pulled up the ladder, and the wooden trap door slammed into place.

At least he left the lights on.

I sank to the floor, trying to take in what had just happened.

I'd told Nick and Kai not to hang around, but I'd had the funny feeling they wouldn't listen.

Now I hoped to God they hadn't. I'd fight to escape, but for now, they were my best chance.

I paced, alone, with only the faint buzz of the monitor for company. I tested the bars, even banged my shoulder into them, but I was trapped.

Half an hour later, when my father walked into Maddie's room, his eyes went to the camera. He smiled at me.

Then he sat down on the edge of Maddie's bed to wake her. When he spoke, the monitor chimed and then sound clicked on, staticky but audible. She sat up, rubbing sleep from her eyes, as he patted her knee.

He told her I ran away from home.

He told her I left them both.

And when she curled up in his arms, sobbing desperately, she couldn't see the way he smiled over her shoulder. I screamed at the monitor, but it was a one-way feed, and I reached out through the bars so desperately that I bruised my shoulder, but I couldn't get to it.

When my panic faded, as my sister sniffled and wept, unreachable, then despair curled around me. I raised my chin, trying to fight it.

I was a princess, even if I was lost and imprisoned.

He thought I was the princess of nothing.

But I knew better.

I'd always been a princess, no matter what was done to me. I always would be.

And I'd fight for my sister and my kingdom.

23

Kai

"We can't just leave her," Nick said.

"Callum wanted us to bring the car home and *then* double back," I said. It was the smart choice. Leaving the car on a nearby street might draw attention. Especially in Piper's neighborhood, where everyone parked in their big garages or in their long driveways. Our car parked on the street would stand out. Piper's father might notice, and then we'd have made more trouble for her. And Callum was worried about even more dangerous enemies.

Nick looked out the window, watching the big houses on the rolling green lawns. He didn't feel right leaving Piper, even for ten minutes, but he didn't argue with me.

I took the turn onto the main road that led toward town, then took the next right, a quiet country road. Nick's head snapped toward me, and his eyebrows rose. I didn't say anything as I pulled over into the gravel at the side of the road. As I rose out of the driver's side, I stripped off my hoodie and tossed it on the driver's seat before pulling off my white t-shirt. I'd use it to mark our car as disabled. Hopefully it wouldn't draw too much attention while we doubled back to check on her.

I had an itchy feeling. And I also hated that the kid felt uneasy. He should learn to trust his instincts, too.

"Thanks," Nick said to me.

I rolled the white t-shirt up in the window, and the breeze caught it and set it flapping like a flag. "Let's go check on our girl."

Together, the two of us headed through the woods at a run. Every once in a while, Nick would stumble, breaking the near-silence of the woods as a branch broke or as he caught himself with a hand against a tree. Sometimes, because Nick was big and quiet and well-spoken when he did talk, it was easy to forget he was the youngest, and he hadn't grown fully into himself yet. As a man or as a werewolf.

The stretch of woods just beyond Piper's lush, freshly-clipped backyard was familiar now, from the fallen tree with moss growing across its side to the long-abandoned deer hollow filled with damp leaves. I leaned against one of the trees. Even in human form, our hearing was powerful enough that we'd hear raised voices if Piper had trouble with her father.

"When do you think we'll get to hunt some witches?" Nick asked.

That was a hell of a way to make small talk. I grunted.

The night he'd shifted and lost his humanity, streaking off through the woods, I'd been so pissed. At myself, and at Callum, not at Nick. We'd finally found each other, and I didn't want to lose any pack-members because we did a bad job teaching him how to be a wolf. Callum said he'd be fine, but he hadn't been the one who was right there, trying to guide him. I felt tense and irritated every time Nick shifted. Never knew when things might go wrong.

But, the only way out was through it. At least Nick had help as he learned to shift. I'd been alone.

"Do you think they're all bad?" he mused. He sat on the downed tree, resting his elbows on his knees. "Or just the ones in that coven?"

"Don't know," I said. "Maybe I'll be more curious about the rest of them after we've destroyed this coven."

Nick rubbed his hand across his face. "I just—"

Whatever Nick was *just* was lost as Piper cried out. He jumped forward, already rushing the treeline, and I grabbed his arm to yank him back. I flashed him a warning look. We had to be smart to help Piper. But as soon as he paused, nodding that he was under control, I signaled to indicate we should move to the edge of the house. The two of us loped quickly across the wide-open lawn to the corner of the house.

Inside, Piper's voice rose in something between a scream and a cry. My heart lurched, then anger swept over me. The first frantic rush of fear was replaced with the cold desire to hurt someone. I signaled Nick to wait, while I paused at the big dining room bay window. Sometimes the only way out was through, and sometimes, the only way *in* was through. I didn't want him cutting himself on the glass. I'd go in first.

Piper fell quiet. I ran back across the grass and turned, steeling myself for the running jump that would carry me through.

Piper screamed, one last time, and there was a *thud* like a trunk being slammed shut. A car engine started, and the garage door began to rumble.

"Fuck!" As I ran for the garage, I whipped the words over my shoulder. "Call Callum, we need backup. Now."

Nick stood rooted to the spot, wide-eyed. I glanced him out of my peripheral vision and turned, snarling at him to *call.*

He stared down at his hands, hands which were beginning to twist and deform, claws cracking open his bleeding fingertips.

"Get it together," I hissed. He shouldn't change here. Wolves streaking through the neighborhood would definitely draw attention.

It was up to me to call Callum, and I dialed frantically as Nick fell to his knees. There was a savage tearing sound as his joints reversed, and he made a frantic sound of pain.

"Yeah?" Callum answered the phone.

"Piper's father is taking her somewhere."

"Follow them."

I didn't have the car. I'd fucked this up royally. And Piper was the one who'd pay for all my mistakes.

"I'm going to have to go as a wolf," I said, my voice low and sure. It was the only way I could keep up.

"No," Callum said.

"We lose her otherwise," I said, already tossing the phone into the grass alongside Nick's twisted body. Whatever Callum shouted through the phone, I managed not to hear.

Nick snarled, bouncing up to all four paws. Whatever the price we paid in pain, the adrenaline that came after was worth it.

"Wait for me." My voice came out as a ragged groan that I tried desperately to swallow as my muscles swelled and my clothes burst away from my body.

The world faded, and then it came back brighter, more vibrant, more *clear* than it ever was in human form.

The Lexus was pulling down the street. I raced behind the car and to one side, trying to stay far enough out of sight. Nick matched me, staying by my side as our paws ate up the ground between us and our girl.

Maybe if someone saw us racing through their yards, they would take us for a pair of Siberian Huskies that had jumped their fence, although we were bigger than any huskies. We turned back down that main road, once again, and now there were woods lining the road that we could streak through. If I could get through to Nick, he could turn off and get the car, but he was snarling, all animal. He was too far out of reason right now. And I couldn't go myself because someone had to be in control, following Piper.

Then the car took the on ramp for the highway. We stood there, trembling with energy, for a second at the edge of the pavement. There was no way we would go unnoticed if we ran along the side of the cement highway. And it was dangerous and terrifying—the loud noises, the terrible smells, humanity everywhere. But if we didn't, we might lose the car.

I growled to Nick, trying to tell him to go through the woods. Hopefully he could scent them.

Then I ran after the car. I heard brakes slam on in panic, near me, cars coming so close that it raised my fur on edge. The cement bit into my paws, but I raced on. The cars were going 65, 70 miles per hour, and the Lexus kept gaining on me. I pushed myself to the limit, as my heart beat frantic in my chest, my breathing coming so short that I tasted the sting of iron at the back of my throat.

And I lost them anyway.

Furious with myself, I stopped and tried to catch Piper's scent, but I only breathed in exhaust fumes.

Callum's truck stopped beside me. Josh jumped out, making a show of talking to me, glancing down the road as if he hoped someone was watching. He let down the tailgate and jumped up himself, patting his leg. "Come on, boy. Get in the car."

I jumped into the metal bed of the pickup truck and Josh slammed it shut. Then the three of us took after, speeding fast toward wherever Nick was. I hoped he'd kept the trail.

"It's all right," Josh said. "You did your best."

He touched my paws, which were torn and bleeding. "Going to stay in form?"

I growled. I didn't want to be human now. I wanted to rip Piper's father from limb to limb.

"We'll find her," he promised. "Somehow."

24

P*iper*

I'D EXPECTED to be alone for a long time, so I was surprised by the sound of feet on the floor ahead. Could it be Nick and Josh and Kai and Callum?

"I'm down here!" My voice came out hoarse, and I tried again. "I'm here!"

The feet paused, and then there was a creaking sound as the trap door was opened.

My father came down the ladder. "I know, Piper." His voice was amused. "You're right where I left you, aren't you?"

"What are you doing here?"

"You're not happy to see me? Soon you'll be glad for any company." He had a leather backpack over his shoulder, and he threw it onto the table. "I have to get that collar off you. That's the only reason I'm here, Piper."

He always said my name so snidely. God, Callum would be able to answer so many questions for me, now that I knew who I was. Well, I didn't know *who* I was.

I knew I was theirs. The pack's. And they were mine.

"You hid me," I said quietly. "Just in case, didn't you? Piper's never been my name."

"Don't ask me what it is," he said. "You weren't talking when I plucked you out of your mother's arms and stepped over your father's body."

A twinkle shone in his eye. I'd known him to be cruel, but not so casually. He'd always been angry before, self-righteous. Now he was amused as I went quiet, just for a second. I had so many questions, but my brain was spinning too fast to form clever questions, questions that wouldn't give away Callum and Josh and Nick and Kai. Instead, I kept imagining things that might have happened, that were suddenly so strong they felt almost like memories: being carried in my mother's arms, my mom whispering *sh, sh* to me as my father transformed outside the door, the shining eyes of a wolf looking over me.

Lucky me, he filled the silence. "I did a good job hiding you, just in case," he said. "There were no birth records for you—you'd been born at home, in the pack house—and so I stole your friend Misty's records. And I put some badly forged records in Misty's name. That way if another pack came looking for you, they'd see just the ordinary, pathetic little girl I've always known."

"And then you stole Maddie," I said. "She would have been four or five? She would have had memories..."

"Not anymore," he said.

"Are they gone forever? Or could her memories come back?"

"Look at you. Always scheming. You're like a determined little rat."

I guessed there were worse things to be than a rat, such as a human who would destroy countless lives and tear apart families for a chance at more power.

"So this it?" I asked him. "You stole my magic so you could own a factory and some luxury cars? You don't want to run for president or *do* something…"

"I've had to share the magic with those who helped me gain it," he said. "But I understand why Alan would try to seize all the power for himself. Your power could be harnessed by just one person for bigger, better things. It's amazing we've lived this long in harmony, dominating Blissford and the state of Virginia." He shook his head, as if he was surprised by their virtue.

As he spoke, he was setting up a bowl on the countertop, building a small fire in it, sprinkling in herbs. I didn't dare ask if he had blood to break the spell; I had to keep the guys a secret so they would be safe. And hopefully, eventually, they would find me, if I didn't save myself first.

"What are you doing?" I asked.

"A spell to remove that necklace," he said. "I would hate for Alan to find you while you were still bound to his allegiance."

"It doesn't seem like the worst thing from my perspective," I said drily.

"Turn around and back up to the bars," he instructed me. He pulled a cardboard box with holes in it out of his backpack, and I shuddered when I realized there was something alive in there.

"What are you doing?"

"True magic requires blood," he said as he drew a small brown mouse out of the box. "So many people don't have the stomach to reach out and take the power available to them."

God, he was such a self-satisfied prick.

"You don't want to watch this," he said. "Put your back against the bars, like I told you."

I was never going to willingly turn my back on him, and instead I pressed my spine against the rough plywood wall. But I did close my eyes, though it did little to help. Between the small desperate sounds and my own imagination, I saw more than I ever wanted to.

"Up against the bars," he said impatiently. "I need contact to get this necklace off you."

"Is it going to hurt?"

"Yes," he said, without hesitation. "But so will being shot in the knee. Last warning, Piper. Time's a wasting."

He still carried the gun in the holster on his hip. Reluctantly, I came to the bars. As soon as I was close enough, he grabbed me by the collar and yanked me closer. My face slammed into the metal bar, and pain exploded above my eye. Something cool ran down my forehead.

Then those sensations were lost to blinding pain.

I let my legs crumble beneath me—not that I had much choice—and at this awkward angle, he couldn't hold me. He swore as he lost his grip and I tumbled to the floor. I hit hard but I made sure I landed with my head and shoulders out of his reach.

Then I played dead.

He stared at me for a long minute. My breathing felt frantic and I tried desperately to look helpless and out of it as the waves of pain radiating from my neck through my head and arms faded into an uncomfortable tingling.

"Piper," he said. "I've got half a mind to shoot you and see what happens. If you're faking, best get up now."

I groaned in response, slurring my words, trying to tell him I couldn't stand.

Then, reluctantly, he drew his gun and unlocked the cell door. He held it on me as he knelt beside me, reaching out to grab the necklace. I made myself wait as he leaned over my body, as his fingers neared my throat.

And I exploded into life.

I slammed myself into him. *The gun, get the gun.* Nothing else mattered but knocking that barrel toward the ceiling. His finger wasn't in the trigger well and the gun flew toward the far wall. The two of us scrambled to our feet, pushing against each other as we raced for the gun on the other side of the cell.

But I was closest to the door. How fast could I get up the ladder? Quicker than thought, moving on instinct, I gave up on the gun. I raced out the door, slamming it shut behind me. It banged shut, hard, and clicked.

"Piper!" He screamed, and he'd already reached the gun as I got to the ladder, as I scrambled up. The metal cut into my fingers, my feet slipping on the rungs as I climbed. From the corner of my vision, from my instincts, I knew he was raising the gun, sighting in.

He squeezed off a round, the sound so loud my eardrums popped. It hit near me, splintering plywood, but I fell onto my knees away from the blast, scrambling across the floor of the hunting cabin. I grabbed the trap door and pulled it up on its hinges, then let it go. It slammed shut as the second round went off, punching through the floor to my left.

I ran for the door to the hunting cabin. It was locked, and in my panic, with my trembling fingers, I could barely get the deadbolt open.

And then I was loose, tumbling onto the porch.

The fall day was quiet and sunny. Yellow and red trees mixed with pines, surrounding the cabin as far as the eye could see. His Lexus was still parked in the driveway.

The keys. He probably still had the keys on him.

And he'd have the keys to the damn cage too.

I could have screamed, but there was no time to lose. I had to check the car, as fast as I could, and then get away through the woods if the keys weren't there.

I launched myself across the porch, running hard for the car, then yanked the driver's side door open. There were no keys in the ignition or in the well between the seats—my father usually drove a car with a fob and an automatic start—so I was going to have to figure out where I was and how to get to help.

"God help me," I muttered as I straightened from the car. Should I stick close to the dirt trail leading through the woods? Would it be faster to stay on the trail itself, worth the added danger?

Someone grabbed my shoulder. A voice behind me said, "God's not on your side."

25

I whirled to face Eli. He grinned at me as his fingers sunk bruisingly deep into my biceps.

"That's enough, Eli." His father, Alan, said sharply. He stood behind Eli. "Let the girl go."

Eli squeezed a little tighter before he pushed me away at the same time as he let go. I stumbled against the side of the car before I caught myself.

"Fine," he said. "I don't want the smell of dog on my clothes anyway."

I looked past him to Alan, who frowned at us both. When his gaze flickered to Eli, he looked disappointed.

"Thank you," I said to Alan, cautiously, still trying to estimate my chances of making it if I ran. I was fast, but I was exhausted and aching. I glanced down the long dirt lane that led to a gravel road. We were so isolated.

And I wasn't sure if I *could* run, or if the Kingstons could compel me to turn around and come back. What if I couldn't hear them? What if I plugged my ears when I ran, so even if I had to obey them if I heard, I didn't know what they wanted?

My gaze swept around rapidly, trying to find a way out of this trap.

Alan held his hand out as if he noticed, as if he was hoping to calm me.

And that was when I realized we weren't alone. There were others standing in the shadows of the woods. Once I found the first man standing there, I picked out others. Two men. The judge. The sheriff.

"You're the coven," I said softly. "My father's...friends."

"I am no friend of your father's," Alan said. "He's power-hungry and dangerous, Piper. You of all people know that."

"I do." He was hardly the only one to suffer from those tendencies.

The man in front of me seemed kind enough right now.

But it didn't escape my attention that I was surrounded.

That didn't make me feel friendly.

"We had to stop him," Alan said. "Is he...in the house?"

"Yes."

"Did you kill him?"

There was a quickness in his speech that made me think he'd like it if I had.

"No," I said. "I didn't...I trapped him in the cell."

Alan's lips parted in a grin. "You did, huh? And here he always prides himself on being the smartest person in the room."

I glanced again at the figures in the shadows. "So, I've helped you get what you wanted, apparently."

There was no point now in pretending I didn't know who they were.

"It's a complicated situation, Piper," Alan said.

I skated my fingertips over the raised edges of the necklace. Pain tingled along my throat, but it was a gentle throb as long as I didn't press harder. Still, I could feel the cuts and bruises on my skin from where my father had yanked on this necklace as if I was in chains. "I'd like it if you took this off, please."

"I can't do that," he said gently. "But I'd like the chance to explain why to you."

"Are you the one who worked this spell?" I had to know, if I was going to get free.

"It doesn't matter." His eyes were intent on mine as he shouldered his son aside and extended his hand to touch my forearm comfortingly. "What matters is there is more going on than you can possibly see, Piper. More than your father would ever have told you."

"You are the one who enchanted me," I said, gambling on it. "And you didn't put this on me to make sure I'd be Eli's Stepford girlfriend. You *bound* me because you wanted to take the control from my father."

"And keep the power for the many," he said, his voice loud. He must be making sure it carried to those in the forest. "For good causes, Piper. We've done the Lord's work, though perhaps with the devil's pride... and I'm sorry for the harm done along the way."

His gaze lingered on my throat. "But we can get you healed up."

"I don't want to be healed." My voice still sounded raspy from everything I'd been through, but it came out loud and clear. "I want to be free."

"We'll take care of you and your sister," he promised me.

I shook my head.

One of the men—my god, it was one of our state senators—stepped out and said, "It's a good try, Alan, but look at her. She's already been listed as a runaway. It's easier if she stays that way."

Why did I have a funny feeling that *runaway* meant *chained in someone's basement?*

Up until the point that Maddie's power manifested, and then maybe it became *buried under someone's basement?*

My gaze swiveled between Alan and the senator. "I don't want to leave my little sister behind."

It was the truth, but I was using it to stall them, to try to figure out my next move. But the problem with speaking the truth is that there is no time when one's voice shakes more. I sounded so weak, and the sound inflamed my own fear.

How the hell was I going to escape a half dozen witches?

"What is it you want from me?" I asked. "If there's something I can give you, so my little sister and I can be free..."

"What we want, we've already got," Eli said. "We don't have to make you happy, Piper."

"Eli." Alan's voice was stern. "Jesus, boy, you need to learn the art of negotiation. Force does not yield results."

"Sometimes it does," drawled the senator.

Just then, the door to the house was thrown open so hard it slammed against the wall, and my father staggered out. He held the gun in front of him and he pointed it at me for one single-minded second as he stumbled across the porch.

Then he registered Alan, and the barrel swiveled to him.

Alan raised his hands, as calm and unruffled as ever. "Now what?"

He went on talking, but as he did, the boom of my father's handgun filled the air, which was tinged with smoke and the scent of gunfire.

I threw myself away from Alan, who raised his hands, throwing up a shield of magic. As soon as I landed in the dirt, I scrambled under the car. My breathing was loud under the grease-scented undercarriage as I crawled underneath, sliding my legs around so I could see what was happening back in the clearing.

"There you are," Eli was on the other side of the car, his cheek pressing against the dirt as he locked eyes with me. "Come here, Piper."

He waggled his fingers at me, and I shook my head. Eli Kingston could go fuck himself.

And then, as if my arms were operating on their own, I planted my elbow in the dirt and dragged my body toward him, then another elbow. Slowly, despite my brain screaming at my body to stop, I crawled out the other side as he backed up.

"Up, up," he said, gesturing, and I stood. He grabbed my waist, whirling around with me so that my body pressed against his.

Suddenly there was a glint of metal in his hand, then cold steel burning against my temple.

I was getting very, very tired of people pulling guns on me.

Eli called my father's name. "You might want to stop. I'm about to put a bullet through the powerhouse's brain here if you shoot that gun at my father one more time."

Both Alan and the man I'd thought was my father turned, focusing on us. Using me as his shield, Eli maneuvered us around the car.

"Put the gun down," Eli said. Into my ear, he murmured, "Look at you, peacemaker. You're all kinds of useful."

"I don't think so," my father said. Apparently, Eli had gotten ahead of himself. "I'd rather the girl was dead than yours."

I really regretted ever making him a Father's Day card.

Eli's breath curled against my cheek. But whatever he was saying was lost as I saw the faintest flicker of movement in the forest across from us. The humans were behind us, watching the battle play out, perhaps more interested in maintaining their power than being on any particular side. But there was someone else coming.

Were the wolves finally coming to rescue me?

"Are you deaf?" Eli snapped at me. Looking up, he asked, "Dad, are you sure this spell took?"

My father's gun swiveled to me and Eli. "I'm about to shoot you both and make this world a much less whiny place."

Another gun went off, a sharp retort that broke open the day. If these people loved magic so much, why didn't they use it instead of bullets?

As gunfire broke out between the two sides of the witchy contingent, I tried to shove Eli away from me, but he reeled me back against his body. "Uh-uh. You're going to do your best to keep me alive." His grip tightened on my waist, punishingly tight. His lips grazed my ear when he said, "Promise."

My four wolves swarmed the clearing. My father went down hard, the gun flying away from his hand. In the forest, someone screamed. Another wolf hit Eli and me, knocking us both down. I rolled across the ground, then scrambled to my feet, running for the tree line.

The guys and I needed to get out of here, away from the danger of being shot or caught in some magical crossfire.

"Piper!" Eli's voice was a whip-crack I couldn't ignore. "Pick that gun up."

I turned back, trembling. The fight raged around us, but all I could see was the boy I hated, pinning beneath the paws of a growling wolf. Eli's eyes locked on me, then flickered meaningfully to my father's gun, lying in the grass.

I couldn't resist. I bent low and ran across the ground to pick up the gun. It felt heavy and awkward in my hand. My father had always owned guns when I was growing up, but he never took me shooting or let me near them. I'd seen them, from a distance when he cleaned them or carried them to the range, but I'd never touched one.

"Now kill this goddamned wolf," Eli said.

The wolf growled and, quick as instinct, he sunk his teeth into Eli's throat. Eli screamed, and the scream faded into a harsh burble as the wolf tore his throat out.

Which of my wolves killed Eli Kingston? I didn't know. I wasn't sure I ever wanted to know.

But, against my will, my arms extended, my elbows locking, the barrel rising toward the wolf.

Green eyes, framed by black and then surrounded by fluffy white fur, met mine and widened.

My finger slid into the trigger well, brushing over the cool metal. I tried to straighten my finger out, to drop the gun, but it stuck to my palm. Hot tears blurred my vision as I tried desperately to fight back the compulsion to obey.

Kill the wolf.

Eli had said to kill the *wolf*.

"Change!" I screamed at the wolf. *Please trust me.* "Change back!"

He cocked his head to one side, as if he didn't understand. Oh my god, it was Nick, that was Nick's mannerism, those were Nick's vivid green eyes.

My hands trembled so badly that if I fired the shot, I might well miss him. There was a thread of hope. I looked from side to side, desperately searching for someone who could save Nick from me and in doing that, could save us both. I wouldn't mind one of those wolves slamming into me right now.

But the scene around us was still all chaos. Wolves battled witches, fang and claw against sprays of magic and occasional bullets. There was no one else to save me.

Movement in front of me drew my eye. The wolf scrambled in the dirt, as if it were in pain, and then suddenly leaped to its feet. Joints popped out of place and the wolf seemed to shimmer. I couldn't quite make out what was happening in front of me—he was a blur of movement—but I caught glimpses of fur and blood and flesh.

Then Nick was on his knees in front of me. His chest fluttered with the effort of his breath and he raked his hand through his hair, pushing it back from his face, as he looked up at me.

The gun finally fell from my hand.

"Piper," he said, and he was up and at my side, holding me against his chest.

His naked chest.

But still, I wrapped my hands around his biceps, letting him hold my weight. "Nick," I murmured. "We have to get out of here."

"Do you know who bound you?" he asked.

"It's not important," I said. "Not like keeping you safe is."

"Piper, there's nothing more important than making sure you're free," he said. "If you weren't so quick-thinking, I'd be dead because you were bound."

The thought of what had almost happened made my knees feel weak, but I didn't have time for that. I would fall apart later.

"I think it was Alan Kingston, Eli's father." I searched the area for him. He was groaning on the ground, crawling toward a weapon.

Without hesitating, the enormous white wolf streaked across the clearing. Alan got his hand on the gun, whipping his arm around to fire off a shot. The wolf ripped his arm out of the socket, throwing it and the gun aside, and Alan screamed before he slammed into the ground.

The wolf lunged at his throat.

Nick grabbed me in his arms, turning my face to his, as the screaming broke off.

I gasped, the world spinning, as the necklace slipped off my throat. Nick caught me, his arm tightening around my waist. The emeralds dropped from the necklace, disappearing into the grass at our feet, and the chains between the stones dropped away in ashes, scattering to nothing.

"I'm free," I whispered.

Nick grinned down at me, his eyes crinkling at the corners, and I grabbed his shoulders and yanked him down to me. There on the battlefield, surrounded by the wolves of my pack and the bodies of our enemies, I kissed Nick hard.

Because that was what I wanted to do with my freedom.

26

The pick-up truck turned down the familiar pine-lined road that led to the guys' house, and I dared to look over at Nick, who drove.

Thank god he was driving, because the boy was naked and my concentration would have been shot. He caught me looking—even though I quickly jerked my eyes from the distinct shape of his biceps to the road—and cleared his throat. "Sorry."

"Don't be sorry," I said. "I'm sorry."

It was still hard not to glance over at the seatbelt he'd pulled across his lap, at the hard squares of his defined abs divided by the line of gray fabric, or just a little further south.

Blushing, I turned to look out the window into the bed of the pickup truck. Three wolves lay in the bed of the pickup, staying low to avoid attention, but the wind ruffled their fur.

"Can you tell which one is which?" Nick asked.

I studied them all carefully. "The big, angry one is Callum."

Nick nodded. "True in any form."

"The also-kind-of-big one with all the gray is Josh," I glanced at him to see if I was right, and was rewarded with the faintest nod. "And then the small—but I bet fierce—one is Kai."

"You've got us all figured out."

"Thank you for trusting me and changing when I asked you to," I said. It meant a lot to me.

"I'm just happy I understood you," he said, as if it was nothing for him to listen to me, as if it just made sense. That wasn't how the men in my life treated me before I met the pack, and it filled my chest with a warm glow. He went on, "Normally, even though I'm still human in the wolf form, it's hard for me to process language. It all seems so muted, it kind of blurs together in one note. But I understood you."

"Because I'm the pack princess, maybe?"

His eyes widened. "Piper..."

"I'm not Piper," I said. I glanced back at the bed of the truck. "We're almost home. Maybe I should explain it then."

"Okay." A smile tugged at the edges of his handsome mouth, but he seemed to fight it.

"What's going on?"

"Home," he said. "You called Blissford Pack home."

"Psh. It's just where we're going right now," I said. I wasn't ready to get all sentimental with them. I was still shaking with adrenaline from the fight. And I had a desperate urge to tell them everything, to have someone else know who I was.

I'd gone so many years without knowing.

I was excited to have a real identity for the first time in years. And what an identity. Josh would be thrilled. And Kai, in his own way, too. I wondered if he would say something to be a wiseass, or kiss me. Or both. I'd take both.

When I imagined Callum hearing the news, well, the smile I couldn't resist fell away. I wasn't sure how happy Callum would be about having me be part of the pack.

"I wonder why there seems to be a...pack thing between us all," I said shyly, uncomfortable with using a silly word like *crush* and even more uncomfortable with using any serious words. "Except for Callum."

He shrugged. "Are you sure there isn't?"

"I mean." I'd kissed Nick, and Josh, and Kai. That there was something magnetic between me and them seemed undeniable. But there was nothing like that with Callum. There was just my crush, and my body responding to his combination of *gorgeous* and *athletic* and *caring bossy*. It was nothing like the mutual intrigue between me and the guys.

"Callum plays his cards pretty close to his chest," Nick said. "You might have to actually...talk to him."

"Of course I'll talk to him." I rolled my eyes, glancing at the wolves in the back of the truck again. It wasn't like I was *intimidated* by Callum.

He turned down the driveway, and I felt some of the tightness in my body relax as we parked in front of the big, welcoming house. I felt safe here.

"If you'd give us all a minute," Nick said.

To be human. And *dressed* humans. Okay. I could do that.

I nodded and smiled and slid out of the truck, still feeling a bit shell-shocked. I walked into the quiet, warm house, then wandered into the living room where I'd found myself that first night, the night I'd hit Nick Since hee wore nothing but jeans, with the car, and where I'd tossed and turned in the agony of that fever. This room was full of memories already.

The front door opened, and Josh sped to my side. He wore jeans and a fleece, but his feet were bare, and his messy blond hair was ruffled. "Are you all right?"

"I'm fine," I said, touching his arm. "Thanks to you. Thanks for the rescue."

He said fiercely, "I'll feel better when we know every member of that coven is..."

He trailed off, as if he had realized he was being scary. His eyes gauged my expression. Was he worried what I thought about him? That was sweet, but unnecessary. I thought he was pretty damn amazing

"Squishy?" I supplied.

Josh's face split in a wide grin. "You really are all right," he said, cupping my cheek with his hand.

"I've got so much to tell you all," I said.

But Josh's lips came down on mine, and I kissed him back hard, my hand twisting in his hair. He kissed me with so much warmth, lighting up my body with energy. With each kiss we traded, we pressed even closer together, his chest against mine so tightly that I could feel the rapid beating of his heart. I would have sworn his heart raced more when we were close like this than it had in the fight.

The door flew open and Kai ran in. "Piper..."

The word died on his lips when he saw me pulling away from Josh. I worried he was offended, but a few quick steps brought him to us, and then he wrapped his arms around me from behind. He pressed his cheek against mine and breathed in deeply, as if he was breathing in my scent. "I'm so sorry."

I caught his cheek with my hand, turning my face into his. "You don't have anything to be sorry for."

There was that familiar ornery look in his eyes. "I lost the car. I was trying to follow you..."

"You stayed at the house when I went in and ran into my father," I filled in. They were always watching over me. "Well, not-my-father."

"We realized you were in trouble, but we couldn't catch the car."

"It's all right," I said softly. "We're all here. Alive. That's all that matters."

"You got hurt because I didn't protect you," he muttered. "I can't stand it."

My eyes flickered to Josh. "Well, you might have to get used to it. What did you say, Josh? There's nothing safe in the world of witches and wolves?"

"Yeah?" Josh's eyebrows arched. "I hope you'll stick around in our world, Piper. But I'm not looking to keep you in danger, either."

Kai's arm tightened around my waist possessively. "Maybe Callum is right. You'd be safer without us."

I shook my head. "No, I belong here with you."

Kai growled softly, under his breath. I thought he was angry, and then his lips pressed just below my ear. As he devoured me with kisses, I realized it was a growl of desire. "Even after all that, you want to stay with us?" he murmured between kisses.

I should have been able to answer him intelligently. But I was pinned between the two beautiful boys, as Kai peppered my shoulders and neck with kisses, as Josh's lips pressed again to mine. The sensations, and their warmth, and the woodsy, pleasant scent of their bodies overwhelmed me and chased away all conscious thought. I felt as if I floated between them as their powerful arms held me, as I traded kisses with them both, as my hands drifted across the hard-angled lines of their bodies.

Kai's words still bothered me, and I kissed his cheek, trying to think of what to say to make him feel better.

Callum burst in, followed by Nick. Callum's gaze flickered to the three of us as we disentangled ourselves and smoothed our clothes. He shook his head, but said nothing.

Even as I tucked my hair behind my ears and tried to look unruffled, I was touched that Kai and Josh wanted me, even though they thought I was nothing special to their pack. I wanted to talk to Callum one more time before I told him that I was the one he was looking for.

"It worked," Callum said, with relief evident in his voice as his gaze fell on my neck. "The enchantment died with the enchanter."

I rubbed at the bruises and marks across my skin, feeling how tender it was, and Callum frowned. I let my hand fall to my side. I was fine, or at least, I would be.

"I have to get my sister," I said. Then it dawned on me she could be in danger too. "Oh my god. What if there's more of the coven? What if my dad made it out alive?"

"Your father did not make it out alive." Callum stepped forward, cupping my face with his hands. His face was grave and sorrowful. "I hope that doesn't weigh on you too heavily, Piper. But you should know the truth."

"You killed him."

He nodded. "I did."

He didn't pretend to regret it.

"I have a feeling Piper's right and there's more to the coven," Josh said. He held out a leather-wrapped journal. "I took this off one of the witches. It's written in code, but I swear there are names here. Lots of names."

"Good," Callum said. "The entire coven would have been responsible for the powerful enchantments binding Piper. The necklace might be gone, but there are more..."

"So I won't shift?" I asked. I'd tried to make the words sound casual, but the thought that there were still witches out there, draining my magic, gave me a creepy feeling running up my spine.

"We'll protect you until you can," Josh promised.

"Let's go." Callum pulled me out the door, toward his truck, and the other three headed for the car. Together, we all raced down the roads toward my childhood home.

I chewed on my lower lip as I leaned forward, watching the trees flash by. Callum was driving fast, but I still couldn't stand the wait. What if they had my sister?

"It's going to be okay," Callum promised, daring to take one hand off the wheel despite his speed, to rest it on my leg.

"I want to be able to protect her," I said softly.

"You will," he said. "You *have*. Even without being able to shift."

"But I will," I said softly. "Soon. Right?"

His lips tightened. "Yes," he said, but this time, I could tell he was lying to me. He wasn't sure we'd break the spells soon at all.

I would've felt despair, but we crested the hill that overlooked the ridiculous houses on their big green squares, and I could see my home. We raced toward it and Callum pulled in the driveway. The guys' car pulled in behind us.

Callum jumped out of the car and tilted his head back. "I don't smell anything off."

I ran for the house, and he matched my pace easily. When we reached the front door, I flung it open and ran up the stairs.

Maddie came out of her room, her eyes wide. Her television was on, playing a movie in the background. When she saw me, she threw herself into my arms.

"Oh, Maddie." I squeezed her tight. "Are you okay?"

"Where've you been?" she demanded.

"It's a long, long story, but I'm going to explain it all to you," I promised. I buried my head in her hair. "It's your story too."

27

The rest of the day was spent making sure Maddie felt safe. She had been through a lot, and as much as I wanted to sit down and talk to the guys, my first priority was making sure that she was okay. We went for a long walk through the forest—I had the funny feeling we were shadowed by watchful wolves, though I never saw them—to the edge of the river where we skipped stones. We didn't talk about anything; I just wanted to be there for her.

The guys got Chinese take-out for us all for dinner, and had her laughing at the ridiculous quantity of food they ordered. She sat at the coffee table, her legs crossed, eating sweet-and-sour chicken and staring at the TV, laughing at terrible cartoons that the rest of us suffered through. Or at least, I thought we were all suffering through them, until Josh laughed out loud, and she leaned back against his legs, comfortable as could be, her gaze still fixed on the screen. Josh paused for a second, and then took my hand in his, holding it between us on the couch.

It was going to take time, but we were going to be all right.

That night, I tucked her into one of the spare bedrooms. "I'm going to stay up for a while, but I'll come back and sleep in your room," I promised.

She raised her eyebrows at me. "Really?"

"Maddie!" I said, scandalized.

"What? I'm just being realistic!"

"You can't be that realistic, you're nine," I said, exasperated. Maybe I was most exasperated because my little sister could see right through me.

Well, she wasn't exactly my little sister, at least not the way we'd thought. We'd have to deal with that another day. But even though we didn't have the same parents, she couldn't have been more my sister.

She fell back into the blankets with a sigh. When she turned over onto her left side, tucking her arm under her cheek the way she always slept, I knew she was on the verge of sleep. It had been a long, exhausting day for us both. I patted the blanket over her hip and started to stand.

"Piper," she said, her voice catching me. "Was Dad a really bad man?"

"Can we talk about it in the morning?"

"No." Her sleepy voice sounded petulant. "Isn't that an easy question to answer?"

"Whatever Dad was," I said, "it doesn't matter to us. Because we're our own people, and we're safe now."

She was quiet, as if mulling this over, and then I heard the faintest soft snore.

I tiptoed out of the room, afraid to wake her, and went down the hall. Before I reached the stairs, Callum stepped out of his room. His hair was wet, soaking the shoulders of his t-shirt, as if he'd just left the shower.

"Piper," he said, his voice hushed. "How is Maddie?"

"Probably in need of many years of therapy," I said. "Just like me. But she'll be fine."

"Of course she will. She's tough like her sister."

So Callum didn't know. I was almost surprised Nick had kept my confidence, but maybe I shouldn't be. He seemed like the type of guy I was safe with in every way, right down to secrets.

"Can I talk to you for a minute?" I said.

A resigned look crept over his face. "Okay. Come on."

I wanted to know what that look was for, but Callum turned and led me down the hall, the opposite way I expected. At the end of the hall there was a narrower set of stairs that led down to the kitchen, and to the other side, even narrower stairs that led up. Callum took the dark, narrow stairs easily, but I followed him uncertainly.

Until we emerged onto the roof.

"Widow's walk," he said. "Of course we're inland and there's no reason here, but it give us a view of the forest and any dangers coming our way."

"And it's beautiful," I said, surveying the scenery, which was lovely even under the moonlight.

"Yes, it is." He leaned against the railing, his arms crossed. "What did you want to talk to me about, Piper?"

I was still curious about that look earlier. "What do you think?"

He sighed. "I don't want to play games."

I leaned against the rail beside him, so close that my shoulder almost brushed his. "I don't either."

"Good," he said. "Then let's speak plainly. What do you want?"

It was a brusque question, and at first, I felt irritated. Then, as he regarded me steadily, I realized he was genuinely curious.

"I'm not sure I can have everything I want," I said.

His lips quirked up slightly. "Yes, I'm familiar with that feeling."

I was still trying to think about what Callum might want when he went on, "But why don't you try to explain?"

"I want my sister to have a normal life, which can't happen here in Blissford anymore," I said. "And I want to be free. And I want to…"

He eyed me, waiting for the last word, and despite the flutter of nervousness I felt when he looked at me that way, I made myself say it. "Stay. I want to stay."

His face relaxed, just slightly. "Good."

"Good? I thought you wanted me gone!"

"Yes," he said, "and no. I'm not sure I can have everything I want, either."

"What is it that you want?"

He gazed out at the pines stretching out around us. "You don't know anything about our world, Piper. And even they remember very little."

"Because the guys were so young when the pack was attacked," I filled in.

"Nick was just a baby. Like Misty."

God, now I felt like I was lying to him by not blurting everything out. But if he wanted me here—even when he thought I wasn't important to their pack—then that meant something. I had to know for sure.

"So what do you think is going to happen here?" I asked. "With Misty?"

He ran his hand through his hair. "She seems really happy with her life here in Blissford."

"Yeah, I think she is." Although I was curious how life was going to change with half the town's self-made aristocracy ripped apart by wild animals. Blissford might just be on the map after this.

"With the coven gone, the magic that bound her should be released over time," he said. "If it doesn't happen naturally, then we'll have to break the enchantments. She'll come into her strength and to begin to transform. And we'll be there for her, of course."

"Of course you would." I couldn't imagine them abandoning anyone who needed their help.

"But maybe she won't," he went on. "Maybe having her powers suppressed all this time changed her. Maybe we all changed, and the way the pack used to work isn't the way it should work now."

"Most of all, I don't want to take away her normal life if she doesn't need to lose it." He shook his head. "Especially when the pack seems to have bonded to...someone else."

"Well," I said, "I wouldn't say *the pack*."

"I would," he said.

I gazed up at him, perplexed. He looked down at me with softness in his eyes for once. The temptation to lean in toward him, to raise my lips toward his and see what happened, was so powerful I almost gave in to desire.

To stop myself, I pressed my palm flat against his chest, holding us apart. His eyes flickered down to my hand, then back to my face; his heart thrummed steadily against my palm, speeding up now, and it reminded me of the way his heart had raced when we shook hands for the first time.

"You've looked at me like I was a problem since I came here," I said.

"Oh, you *are* a problem," he said. "I've been trying to keep the three of them focused on rebuilding our pack. And here you come, and all of them turn into lovesick idiots—"

"Even Kai?" I asked archly. "He's still pretty sarcastic."

"Especially Kai," he said. "That's his version of going soft. He was worse before you came into our lives."

"Hard to believe," I muttered.

"—and worst of all," he went on, "the girl that's been accidentally ruining all my plans is strong and smart, beautiful and brave, and as much as I've tried to rein in those idiots, it turns out I'm a fucking idiot too."

My eyes widened in surprise.

"But I've been doing my best," he went on, "to keep you at arm's length. Because I have to take care of them, and the pack, and be the alpha even when I don't really know how. And you're younger than I am, and you need our help, and I shouldn't—"

I didn't want to hear about all the *shouldn't's*.

So I bobbed onto my toes and kissed him. My lips brushed his, tentatively. Heat flooded my cheeks as I wasn't sure if he would reciprocate or not. For a terrible split-second, he was very still.

Then his lips softened against mine, and he kissed me back, very gently.

I pulled back just enough to see his face. His jaw was stubbled, and his amber-brown eyes were warm beneath long, dark lashes.

"And you shouldn't kiss me?" I asked softly. "Because I think you should."

"It's not a kiss that's the problem," he said. "I've worried about what it would mean. I haven't wanted to make you think there was any chance here. Any hope of some kind of...relationship with the pack. Because of pack law."

His voice had hardened, and I pulled away, settling back onto my heels. "Oh."

How foolish I must look, kissing him. Of course his first allegiance would be to the pack, and to what he thought the pack needed. God, I was making this so terribly awkward. When I told him the truth...

"But then I realize, pack law hasn't always served us," he said. "The packs don't talk to each other. They're territorial. And if they weren't, our house could have been warded against magic, and we all would have grown up with pack law. But we didn't."

"And now I don't want to follow the old rules," he said. His eyes were intent on mine. "I want you. The rest, we can figure out in time."

He wanted me. A warm glow spiked through my chest, as I finally understood the way he looked at me. He felt guilty, and he'd been fighting his desire for me.

"So a kiss means something?" I asked.

He nodded, his fingers trailing up the outside of my thigh—his touch electric—until his hand settled on my hip.

Then suddenly he spun us both around, pushing me against the side of the house. He braced one hand above us, holding his body away from me, although he was so close I could feel his warmth. He kissed me sweetly at first, his lips tender. When my lips parted, seeking more of him, he kissed me back more certainly. His body pressed against mine, his leg pressing between my thighs, and I wrapped my arm around his shoulders. I wanted him closer to me. I wanted him as close as he could be.

All the guys were good kissers, but Callum was extraordinary. His every movement was filled with purpose and desire. I ran my hand down his chest, feeling the hard planes of his pecs and then his abs through the soft flannel of his shirt. The two-day growth across his hard jaw tickled my neck before he devoured me with his kisses, pressing his lips to the soft, tender places between my ear and my shoulder, then moving up to nip my earlobe with his teeth. Every kiss made me throb with desire, a little more each time, until I was on fire for him.

I moaned into his ear, helpless to hold it back, and the sound seemed to spur him further. He returned to my lips, his big hand holding my cheek possessively.

"Do you doubt me now?" he asked, his lips a breath away from mine. "My feelings?"

"No," I said.

His forehead rested against mine, as if he was trying to catch his breath. "Damn me to hell, but I want you more than I want to do the right thing. More than I want to be the alpha."

"There could be more than one way to do the right thing," I said softly.

Some of the haunted look in his eyes faded, and his gaze on mine sharpened. "You're right. Of course, you're right."

"Now, that's the sweetest thing a man can say to a woman," I said. It broke the tension, and he threw his head back and laughed.

Callum's grin was such a beautiful flash of happiness when he was usually so tense, and it made me want to kiss him again, so I did. My lips pressed into the spot where his beard stubble almost hid his dimple.

"And the good news," I said softly, "is that I'm the one you've been looking for."

He pulled back, his hands on my shoulders so he could look into my face. His brows knitted together. "What do you mean?"

"The man who pretended to be my father switched my records for Misty's. I was born here, in this house."

He stared at me. "But—"

"On a stormy night, wasn't it?" I asked. "My *father* told me it was a storming night. He knew I would be trouble because there was a lightning storm, as if God himself raged the night I was born."

"Are you sure?" he muttered. His hands caught my cheeks, and he studied my face with intent hazel eyes.

"The pull that I've felt toward you—toward all of you—and that you feel toward me is no lie. The coven did everything they could to disguise who I was, to set up Misty to look like she was the shifter, in case another pack every came looking for her." I shook my head. "But they didn't realize there were survivors. They didn't realize we'd be drawn together, that it would be impossible to deny who we were to each other."

"How long have you known?"

"Just today," I said. "Don't be mad. I knew I'd be your *duty* once you knew. I wanted to see who I was to you, really."

"You're my everything," he said. "And you were before I even understood that."

He tucked my hair back behind my ear. "But what you *aren't* is Piper Sullivan."

"What's my real name?" I asked softly. A connection with my birth parents!

He shook his head, his eyes sad. "In our pack, the baby's name was always announced at a ceremony when they were a week old. Parents spent the first week resting with their baby while the pack took care of their needs, and then after a week, they would introduce the baby to the pack and there would be a big party."

A sudden sense of loss washed over me. "Did my parents name me?"

"I think so," Callum said, his voice kind. "Your father said your mother had chosen a name. But he didn't tell us what it was."

I nodded. "Well, that's all right."

But Callum's handsome, hewn face went blurry, and suddenly he clasped me tight to his chest, hugging me. His warm, hard arms held me close, as I heard myself make the faintest small sob.

"I'm so sorry," he murmured into my hair.

"It's all right," I said again, but my voice broke. It wasn't convincing at all.

Callum scooped me off the ground, and my arms closed around his shoulders as he lifted me against his chest. I blinked at him in surprise, but he sat down gracefully, with me in his lap. He held me, but I didn't cry for long. Tears had never gotten me anywhere before.

A few strands of hair stuck to my face. Callum tucked them

behind my ear, the gesture quick and fond. "I'll tell you everything I remember about them, I promise."

I nodded, trying to smile. He rubbed his thumb across my cheekbone, gently swiping away the last tears. "You don't have to pretend to smile with me. I'm here for your sadness too. I'm here any way you need me."

I laid my head on his shoulder. The stars seemed so bright out here, in the forest. They were brighter than they ever looked from my father's house.

Well, not my father. I didn't have to think of him that way anymore.

Callum's breath came out softly against my hair. "Well, do you want to go tell each of them who you really are? It seems like a discussion to have one-on-one."

"Yes," I said.

"And tomorrow," he said, "we should have a homecoming party, and a birthday party for you. We were talking about trying to make up for that awful birthday you had."

"I'd like that," I said.

But was it really the worst birthday I could have, if this was the terrible dark road that finally led me home?

28

I raised my hand to knock on Josh's door, then hesitated. I wanted this moment to be special. He'd be elated to know I belonged with the pack. Or, maybe he already thought I belonged with the pack, and he'd just be elated to know that Callum agreed, and that I did too. Since that first moment I met him, he had been kind and warm and good to me. I hadn't realized how alone I was in my little world, how much I needed someone to take care of me, until he came into my life.

How in the world did I say any of that?

The image that rose into my mind, as if answering my own question, was of shoving him against the wall, covering his lips and the hard angles of his cheekbones in kisses, and tearing his t-shirt over his head.

I bit my lip. Maybe that wasn't a communication method so much as a fantasy I'd had since I met him.

Well, Josh had never minded my social awkwardness before. I tapped my knuckles against his door, two quick raps. They sounded faint in the long hallway. It was a weak knock. If I were a big, scary werewolf, I'd make fun of me.

The door swung open, without a pause or a sound on the other side, and Josh leaned against the doorframe. His tall, powerful body was silhouetted in the doorway, with one hand tucked into his jeans pocket.

"Mm?" he asked.

"You were expecting me," I accused.

"I was," he said. "And then, you know, I can smell *and* hear you when you lurk outside my door for three minutes. What was that about, Piper?"

His smile was teasing, but gentle. He really wanted to know. There was a faint dimple of a frown between his eyebrows, too. Maybe he was worried I was leaving them.

As if these guys could ever get rid of me easily. I'd never leave them if I had a choice.

"I wanted to talk to you," I said.

He stepped back, holding his door open for me, and I followed him into his room. Just like I had that first night, the same day I met him.

"The suspense is killing me." Despite the words, when he turned around, his hands were in his pockets and his posture was as straight but relaxed as usual. He seemed cool, and yet I was sure he meant it.

"Didn't Callum talk to you yet about my birthday party tomorrow?" I asked. "I'm not really sure about his party-planning skills. He definitely is going to need help."

Josh quirked an eyebrow, looking at me as if he was waiting for the punchline. I never got much past him.

"Well," I said. "Part belated birthday party. My eighteenth *really* sucked. It could use a do-over. And part..."

"Mm?"

"Part homecoming," I blurted out.

I stared at him, expecting his face to be overcome by surprise, but instead one corner of his mouth quirked up. "Welcome home, princess."

"You knew?" I demanded.

"I had a funny feeling." He took my hand in his, swinging it between us, and then raised it to his mouth. When his lips pressed against my palm, it sent intimate tingles pulsing through my body. "Kai and I talked about it. The bond between us. Your hearing, your strength."

"I see."

"The only thing that made sense..." His eyes met mine as he kissed the inside of my wrist, and the wave of desire that washed over me caused me to draw a quick breath in. "...is that you belong with us. With *me*."

"Oh? And how do you feel about that?" I asked, my lips quirking, my tone light.

"I feel like you're fishing," he said, his smile just as teasing. He began to kiss the inside of my arm again, but even though he was finding erogenous zones I never knew existed, I wanted the night I'd envisioned. I caught the back of his neck with my hand, leaning in toward him, and his big hands wapped around the waist.

"I feel..." His lips met mine, gentle, tasting me. "That you know damn well how I feel."

"No words needed?" I asked the question, but then drew his lower lip into mine, making it near impossible for him to respond.

"Is that why you were in the hallway, stalker?" He teased, his lips nuzzling the corner of my mouth. "Looking for the right words?"

I hooked his collar with my finger, drawing his head down toward me so I could press a kiss to his jaw, which was stubbled with five o'clock shadow after the long day we'd had. It felt nicely scratchy when I kissed him. "I guess maybe words are overrated."

"Maybe." He paused, cupping my face with his palms. Suddenly, the teasing dropped away, and his deep blue eyes were earnest as he gazed into mine. "You know that even if you weren't the pack princess, I would have wanted you, right? I would've chosen you."

"Yes." My whisper was so soft it was barely audible. I hadn't wanted him to choose me over his pack, knowing how much they all needed each other. I'd been willing to sacrifice the love and warmth I felt here to protect them. But the sense of gratitude and relief that washed over me now made my eyes fill with sudden tears. I didn't have to run away from them for their own good. I could stay. I hadn't admitted to myself how much I wanted to be here.

"Oh, none of that," he said, swiping his thumb across my cheekbones, catching my tears. "I'm going to do my best to make you happy."

"Oh? How so?"

"We're going to have one hell of a party," he promised me.

"Mm?" I mimicked him. "And what else?"

He laughed and his hands slid from my hips down my thighs. The stroking of his hands sent throbs of desire through my body, and then his fingers sank into my thighs as he lifted me up easily. I wrapped my legs around his waist, catching his shoulders with my hands. I had to laugh at his sudden, sweet attack as he held me against the wall. His lips nuzzled my throat, and my chin lifted, inviting him in.

"I thought I was going to shove you against the wall tonight," I said, my voice soft, because it was strange to admit something so intimate aloud. "If you teased me one minute more."

"Teasing?" His eyebrows quirked over mischievous blue eyes. "Oh, you haven't seen teasing yet, princess."

I laughed as his mouth swept across my throat and shoulder. My arm tightened around his shoulders as he peppered me with kisses, pushing the collar of my shirt aside. The throb between my thighs turned into a desperate aching need, and I turned my face into his dark blond hair, kissing his hard-angled, ruddy cheekbones. He finally looked back to me, and our lips met over and over.

He turned and carried me to the bed. When he laid me down, his every movement was careful. He said he'd known who I was in part by my strength, but he seemed to think I was fragile, too.

Maybe I was. Maybe I was strong and fragile all at once, after everything I'd been through. Maybe Josh and the rest of the pack were the first people in my life to ever see me as I truly was.

He braced himself over top of me, careful to keep his weight off my body as our lips met again. My shirt rode up, and the hem of his t-shirt brushed against my waist.

I tugged on the hem. "This shirt offends me, FYI."

"Oh?" He sat back, one knee braced on either side of my legs. "What did the shirt do to you?"

"The same thing it did to you. I thought you hated shirts," I said innocently.

"It's just another layer between us and the wolf." He drew his t-shirt over his head, and revealed his chiseled abs, powerful, tattooed pecs, and the sexy rippling of his biceps as he tossed the shirt over his shoulder. "Better?"

"Much."

His fingers swept over the bare skin in the gap between my t-shirt and jeans. "I'm not particularly keen on your shirt, either. FYI."

"Then take it off me." I felt the small, dirty smile turning up my lips. I'd never have imagined I would be so bold with a guy. But...it was Josh. I was safe with him, to be whoever I was.

His eyes crinkled at the corners. What was he up to? Then he bent, brushing his lips over that gap of skin in a tender kiss that made my abs contract and flutter. He took the hem of my t-shirt in his teeth and dragged it up. I breathed in, aroused and curious, and sat up on my elbows. He dragged the shirt up until cool air brushed my skin, and then one of his big hands slid across my breast, caressing it, his thumb sliding under the cup of my bra. My breath gave at the feel of his thumb brushing my nipple, and his lips quirked around his teeth that still held the hem of my shirt.

I sat up, raising my arms over my head, and he rose to pull my shirt over my head entirely. He whipped his head, tossing the shirt halfway across the room.

"And here I was worried for a second you were going to tear it off me," I teased.

"It's on the table," he said. "I figured I needed both my hands to make you happy."

"Oh?" I asked, and then his thumb caressed my nipple again, and I sagged back onto my elbows. His other hand slid between my thighs, caressing me over my clothes until that ache turned into a *fire*.

"It turns out," I managed, putting my hand over his, "that I, as a werewolf myself, actually hate pants."

"*Everyone* hates pants," he informed me.

The backs of his hands brushed across my abs as he worked the button and zipper on my jeans, then dragged my jeans and underwear down my legs. A moment of self-consciousness flashed over me—I was letting this man see me naked—and then was lost to my desire for him.

He stood from the foot of the bed to pull the jeans off my ankles, and tossed them on the foot of the bed. His hands went to his belt—and then he paused.

"Are you sure, Piper?" he asked me. "We can take this as slow as you need to."

"Slow's not what I need right now." My voice came out low, threaded with desire.

"Good." His tone was full of relief. He stepped out of his jeans, revealing the hard muscle of his lower abs, a faint dark blond happy trail, and then the bobbing of his long, thick cock. Despite his obvious desire for me, he added, "We can stop whenever you want, Piper. You can always change your mind. I want this to be good. Special."

It was *special* because it was him.

But I couldn't say something that cheesy.

Instead, I crooked a finger at him, beckoning him toward me.

He threw himself onto the bed beside me, landing with a bounce on his elbow. Those deep blue eyes met mine, and he leaned forward, pressing his lips to mine again. I savored the way he tasted as his lips parted. Tentatively, the tip of his tongue traced the inside of my upper lip. Throbbing for him, I threw my leg over his hip. I just wanted to press myself against him, to have him warm all the empty places within me.

He slid his palm over the curve of my waist to my hip. "This might be easier if you're on top. For the first time."

I nodded and, as he rolled over onto his back, I climbed on top of him. I would've felt shy, uncertain what to do, but he couldn't hide his smile as he gazed up at me like I was the most beautiful thing he'd ever seen.

I wrapped my hand around his cock. "Like this?" I asked innocently, pressing his tip against my core. The second I rubbed his cock against me, it somehow both satisfied the throbbing desire I had for him...and made me want more.

"Yes. You're so wet for me," he murmured, his voice full of wonder.

I drew him in circles across my throbbing core, and felt him groan in desire, as I teased us both now.

"Hang on," he managed, reaching across the bed to fumble open the dresser drawer. He pulled out a condom, and flashed a rueful smile my way. I sat back on his thighs as he ripped open the package and rolled it on. "No wolf cubs for us."

I took him in my hand again. This time, when he brushed between my thighs, I carefully sank down, letting him inside me. I drew in a sharp breath as his tip stretched me, and his lips parted, breathing in too. I grinned, amused that this first step had both of us gasping.

"You feel so damn good," he muttered, his hands tightened around my hips.

With my knees against the hard muscles of his waist, I sank lower. Halfway down, I paused, getting used to the incredible full feeling of having him inside me. It was *almost* painful, almost overwhelming... but so good at the same time.

"You're doing so good, princess," he murmured, and it was his time to crook a finger at me. I bent at the waist, covering his mouth with mine. His fingers wrapped around the back of my head, sinking into my hair, as we traded kisses. He nuzzled the corner of my mouth. "Does it hurt?"

I turned my head, catching his lips with mine. "What really hurts is *not* having you inside me."

He smiled against my mouth. We kissed over and over, until the ache of him filling me had faded. Pulling away from his kiss, even though he half-rose onto his elbows to follow me, I straightened, flashing him a smile. He gazed up at me, his eyes lidded with desire and affection.

I rode him, rising up until he brushed between my thighs, then sliding down until his cock filled me completely and my thighs met the hard muscle of his abs again. Deep heat flushed my body as we moved together. He held my hip in his hand, his fingers as hard and hot and individual as a brand on my ass, and the other hand twisted the bedsheets as he resisted his orgasm. He bit his lower lip, hard, and warmth filled my chest. *I did that to him. He wanted me.*

And the heat rose. My core pulsed around him, and I leaned back, my breasts rising toward the ceiling as my back arched. He took my breast in his hand, his thumb stroking over my nipple, and I almost screamed at the intense sensation.

Together, we came, and I felt him shudder inside me as I tightened around him, over and over, the intense heat fading as pleasure blossomed through every muscle. Then I fell forward onto his chest, and he wrapped his arms around me, holding me tightly, even though he was still buried deep inside me.

He stroked my hair back, then kissed my forehead. The most pleasant ache was between my thighs now, a gentle pain that I didn't mind one bit. I nuzzled my head against his shoulder.

"Don't ever leave me, Piper," he said softly.

I wouldn't. I needed him. But I didn't want to say that, so I just smiled. "As if you could get rid of me."

"I need you," he said, kissing me again.

I didn't entirely believe that this tough, powerful guy needed me, but it was clear he wanted me, and that was enough. He smiled at me fondly, and the two of us curled together.

As the heat between us softened into warmth, I relaxed, safe in his arms.

29

When Callum leaned back in the kitchen chair and tented his fingertips together, it gave me a bad feeling.

"Is it too soon to get back to normal life?" he asked.

Kai snorted, throwing his napkin on top of his plate and scraping back from the table to carry it to the sink. "When have we ever had a normal life?"

"I thought maybe you guys could go to school today," he said. "The Kingstons are gone. Piper's father. I don't want to draw any more suspicion toward us than we have to…"

"It might be good for Maddie," I said. "She's always liked school."

"Wait, wait, wait." Nick had been leaning back, his chair balanced on its back legs, and now he leaned forward, the chair landing with a thump. "You mean you want us to keep going to high school?"

"Until the end of the year." Callum met his eyes evenly. "Piper needs to finish."

"It's a waste of her time and power, not to mention—" Nick began.

"That part is not under negotiation," Callum said. "The only thing we're discussing is whether you go back today or tomorrow."

Callum glanced around the table, meeting the guys' eyes in turn. Kai groaned as he gripped the back of his chair, but he nodded.

Finally, Callum's eyes met mine. One eyebrow arched over his hazel eyes.

"I'm fine with going back today," I said. The truth was that I wanted to graduate; I wanted as normal a life as possible for Maddie and me, at least for now. I still didn't know what it really meant in the long term to be the pack's princess. "If you're going to hell, might as well not procrastinate."

Callum was being the bad guy here, making us all go back. And even though he was being bossy, once again, I was grateful for it.

Callum nodded. "I have the day off work. While you're at school, I'll move your stuff and Maddie's from your father's house."

The thought of going back into that house made a shiver run up my spine. "Thank you."

He nodded. "Of course. Now—go get ready. All of you."

An hour later, after we'd dropped Maddie off at school, Kai cut the engine in the school parking lot. He sighed and put his forehead down on the steering wheel.

I clapped his shoulder. "Buck up. You're practically a god in this school now."

"It's still high school," he said into the steering wheel. "I already did this. It wasn't fun the first time."

"Now you get to do it all over again with me. Maybe it'll be better."

He raised his head and ran his hand through his hair. "Really can't be any worse."

"You know," Josh said, "I was thinking this could be a good thing. We can hear any rumors about the Kingstons and the Sullivans. Control the narrative."

"I appreciate how you're always upbeat," Kai's tone did not suggest sincerity, "but that doesn't change the fact that I have *homework*."

"Like you did that the first time," Josh accused.

Kai considered that, pursing his lips to one side. "Okay, valid point."

Nick swung open my car door and offered me his hand. I took his hand even though I didn't need it, because I liked the feel of his hand against mine. While Josh and Kai, still bantering, scrambled out of the car, the two of us headed for the school steps.

As we reached the wide, concrete steps, Josh came up on my left, resting a possessive, protective hand on my lower back. Kai flanked us to the right, casting a watchful glance around. The students on the steps fell silent except for whispers. In sidelong glances or outright stairs, it felt like everyone watching us. The crowd in front of us melted away.

Surrounded by my guys, we walked into school, and then the crowd folded around us. Everyone wanted to congratulate Josh and Kai on the game, once again, or invite them somewhere, or just say hello. The two of them were busy answering everyone—Josh with his usual golden boy charm, and Kai with grunted one-word answers—as Nick squeezed my hand, smiling down at me.

"I don't care where I am," he murmured, "as long as I'm here with you."

That day at lunch, the four of us took over one of the picnic tables in the yard. It was a warm, sunny day for fall.

"I've got pizza for Josh?" A guy carrying a stack of pizzas glanced around the yard in confusion.

"Right here." Josh gestured to the table.

"You didn't," I said.

"Start as you mean to go on," he reminded me, with a wink. He gestured to the other students hanging out behind the school. "Hey, anyone want a slice?"

I shook my head at him as he lifted out the first slice of pizza and handed it to me. It was fragrant and delicious, and I took a big bite as the chatter and laughter of other students rose around me. They crowded around the table, but I was safe and comfortable, sitting there with my guys, as if we were the center of our own little world.

"Remember our bet?" Josh winked.

I groaned as I tossed my crust back into an empty box. "I hoped you wouldn't."

Just because I'd lost *so* completely. He definitely had gotten the entire school on his side.

"We never defined terms," he said.

"I'm keenly aware."

He slid one finger under my chin, raising it to his eyes. "Well, Piper. I'm defining terms now."

"And what are they?" I raised my eyebrows, trying to look cool, even though when his lips were so near mine, my heart pounded madly.

"I'd like for you to be my girlfriend."

"No fair." Kai threw his pizza crust at Josh's head. "I'll fight you for her."

Josh pursed his lips. "Just *here*. At home..."

Nick shushed them both. He slid his hand across my lower back, tracing small circles. "She's *our* girl."

"Then I guess you guys should've made a bet," Josh said, mock-innocently. "Fine. I'll settle for a kiss."

"You're a scammer—" Kai began.

Josh leaned toward me, and my lips parted, my eyes drifting shut. Everyone else in the world fell away for a second, as Josh's lips pressed against mine in a sweet, chase kiss.

When he leaned away, I opened my eyes and smiled back at him. He looked so pleased with himself. I could pick out the whispers in the crowd, saying that I was the luckiest girl.

They were absolutely right.

A few hours later, I was heading out of my last class when Misty called from behind me, "Hey, Piper!"

She caught my elbow in her hand as I turned. With students streaming around us, she paused, looking as if she was trying to catch her breath. But she didn't have to run that far from Trig. As she seemed to struggle, her cheeks pink, I realized that maybe she just didn't know what to say.

"What is it?" I asked, smiling at her encouragingly.

She took a deep breath. "What happened to us?"

Those words were a swift knife through my chest. "I don't know. We were friends and then we...drifted."

She had drifted, but that wasn't the kind way to phrase it. She hadn't wanted to be my friend anymore.

She frowned. "I know. I just...it felt like one day we were best friends and the next, it felt like you hated me."

"Yeah," I said, frowning back. "That's...how it felt to me. Like you hated me, when you'd been my person for as long as I remembered..."

Callum had felt that there was an enchantment placed on Misty. That was part of why he'd assumed she was the princess, being hidden by the coven using magic. Suddenly, I wondered if the spell on Misty had been for a different purpose. She'd known what happened in my house when we were kids. She'd even talked about how we had to tell someone. She'd fantasized about how maybe her parents would take me in, and we could be sisters...

All the pieces fell into place. Maybe they'd put a spell on her to keep her from trying to help me, to destroy our friendship. And now whoever had put that spell on her—like my father, perhaps—were dead, and so was the magic that had bound her.

"I've missed you." She bit her lip, her gaze flickering down as if she were ashamed. "I wish...things could have been different."

"Well, they can't," I said. "What happened in the past is over."

She nodded, looking glum.

"But in the future?" I asked. "The future can always be different."

Her face brightened.

"Sit with us tomorrow," I said. "We've got a lot of catching up to do."

"We sure do." She bumped her shoulder against mine conspiratorially. "I want to hear all about those guys of yours."

I didn't know if I could tell her *all* about them, but the question definitely made me grin. "Want to watch them practice?" I jerked my head toward the field. "I'm stuck here till they're ready to go."

"It's a sacrifice, watching all those cute boys run up and down the field," she said, "but I'll do anything for you."

We found Nick in the bleachers, sprawling across multiple benches, leaning back on his elbows with a bored look on his face. He was apparently the only person in the school who wasn't impressed by Josh and Kai.

"Hi, Piper and Piper's friend." He patted the bench beside him. I slid in, close to him, my hip pressing his. His hand automatically brushed over the small of my back, sending pleasant tingles along my spine. Misty sat beside me, crossing one leg over the other.

"So this is high school," he mused, staring at the field.

I took his hand in mine, drawing it into my lap. He looked up at me and a smile played across his lips, his gaze full of affection.

"This is high school," I said.

And I couldn't be happier about it.

To read the rest of my adventures in Their Shifter Princess 2: Pack War...

Hi! May Dawson here.

I hope you enjoyed Pack War and you're ready for the wild conclusion of this trilogy in Coven's Revenge!

Join my Facebook community, May Dawson's Wild Angels, where I share excerpts, exclusive content, news and polls!

Thanks for reading!

Best,

May

PACK WAR

"Sorry," I told Kai when we walked into the crowded mall.

"It's fine," he said. "It's not like I hate crowds, or shopping, or...people, really."

He wrapped strong, warm fingers around mine, surprising me. "Come on. What do you need?"

"A new swimsuit."

Kai whistled. "I'm surprised Callum let me take you shopping."

I shook my head. Things were so easy between Josh and Nick and me, but I still felt...outclassed...when it came to Callum. He was just as bad as Kai, in his own way. It was still strange to think of Callum wanting me when he was successful, powerful, and *grown*. I still felt stupid and awkward more often than not.

We passed by an arcade, and I craned my head to peer into the dark interior. "I didn't know there were still arcades!"

"Yep," Kai said. "You want to get your ass kicked at air hockey?"

"Big talk," I said. "I *do* want to kick your ass at air hockey today, actually."

Kai tugged me into the arcade. As he swiped his credit card for tokens, he asked me, "What are you going to give me if I win?"

"It's not going to happen, so there's no reason to discuss it." The trash talk made me feel light and silly.

Tokens rattled out of the machine, and Kai scooped them in his palm. He turned to me with a teasing smile.

"Besides bragging rights," he said, "if I win, I want a kiss."

He could have my kisses, win or lose, but I grinned up at him. "Just a kiss?"

"Oh, it's like that, is it?" he asked, and before I could say anything else, he closed the distance between us, brushing his lips against mine. I caught his big shoulders in my hands, stopping him from pulling away, and he leaned into me as the two of us traded kisses.

When he pulled away, nuzzling the corner of my mouth, I murmured, "And if I win, I get pizza for lunch."

"You're impossible," he said, but kissed me anyway.

During our air hockey game, we traded trash talk and kisses in pretty much equal measure. One game turned into two, and then three, and then we were two-to-two, and I won our fifth game. I raised my arms above my head and twirled, doing a little victory dance that only ended when Kai wrapped his arms around me, stilling me. I tilted my head up to his, my eyelashes fluttering closed, right before he kissed me.

"But I'm the one who won," I murmured when we broke apart.

"You can have your pizza." He ruffled my hair playfully. "You're just so darned cute."

I grinned and ducked my head, trying to hide how nice that was to hear.

He took my hand in his. "Let's go find you some Hawaiian pizza."

I crinkled my nose. "Nope, I'm pretty sure Hawaiian pizza is a sin."

"Oh, I'm sorry, our contract was for *Hawaiian* pizza only..."

As the two of us teased each other, swinging our hands between us as we headed for the food court, I realized that Callum was a genius. I'd never had a playful date like this before with a guy. It felt... nice. And I was grateful that Callum had encouraged—err, ordered—us to take this moment.

After lunch, Kai waited outside the door while I tried on a dozen swimsuits. I debated between looking sexy and feeling confident that I would not have a clothing malfunction. Dressed in a red bikini, I shimmied in front of the mirror, trying to imagine if my breasts would pop out of the cups if I cannonballed into the pool. I'd never cannon-balled in my life, but I wanted to keep my options open. And my cups closed.

I swung the door open and stuck my head out. "What do you think about this one?"

He waved his fingers toward himself, telling me casually to come here.

Then I stepped out of the dressing room, and his eyes widened. "Yeah. Sure. That one."

"It's cute?" I asked.

He sat down on the stool outside the dressing room and leaned forward, propping his elbow on his knee. "Yep."

It wasn't until I retreated back into the dressing room and stripped off the bikini that I realized why he'd sat down right then.

I was grinning when there was a sudden tap on the door. I opened it an inch, and Kai suddenly shoved the door open, pushing in with me.

"Hey!" I said, grabbing my clothes off the bench, embarrassed, but he turned his back to me, looking out through the gap in the door.

"There are wolves in the mall," he said softly. "Another pack, trespassing on our territory. We have to get ready to run."

I hurriedly pulled on my jeans, shoving my feet into my shoes as I zipped the jeans up. "They can't be friendly?"

He shook his head. "Pack is family—but *packs* aren't friends."

I knew that bugged Callum, who felt that the murder of the rest of their pack could have been avoided if the packs had just worked together.

I joined Kai at the door, resting my palm lightly on his back. I inhaled, but I couldn't smell anything strange. For now, my senses were stronger than a human's, but my abilities were still muted by the enchantments that my 'father' had put in place.

"Come on." Kai's worried eyes met mine, and he took my hand again. Together, the two of us snuck out of the dressing room and back into the department store. Racks of colorful clothes spread in front of us, with the fragrance department on the other side. We would have a long walk to either door, either the one to the parking lot or the one to the mall. I stared around, but I didn't see anyone that looked out of place.

"This way," I said softly, and to Kai's credit, he followed me as I made a beeline for the fragrance department in front of us. He groaned when I picked up a bottle of floral perfume, but he still nodded. The heavy scent should help throw any wolves off our tracks.

I quickly doused us both in perfume. Kai turned his face into his shoulder when he sneezed, then pulled away, making a disgusted face. Coughing faintly under his breath, he caught my hand again, and the two of us crept toward the door to the parking lot. He eased his keys out of his pocket and held them out to me.

"If I tell you to run, you run," he told me. "Don't look back. Get back to the house. You'll be safe there."

"I'm not going to leave you," I said. "We'll deal with it together."

"Please," Kai said. "If anything happened to you..."

"What?" I whispered.

Kai's mouth tightened in exasperation. "You want me to talk about my feelings *now?*"

"Like you would if we *weren't* in danger?"

Kai rested a finger across his lips, shushing me.

The two of us reached the glass double doors. A cold blast of air smacked across our faces. Fall was settling into winter.

It was only when we had begun to cross the parking lot that I saw the big guy who stepped between two cars in front of us, blocking our way. When I turned back, I saw two guys in leather—and a tall, leanly muscled woman—who melted out of the shadows to either side of the doors.

Without hesitating, Kai and I juked left and ran, our feet pounding across the pavement.

Their feet were near-silent as we all raced across the parking lot. Cars slammed on their brakes, honking their horns.

Kai pointed ahead of us to our car. "Go! I'll slow them down."

"Kai, no," I begged. "We go together."

"The two of us don't have a chance," he said, his eyes wild. "If you get out of here and get Callum, I might make it."

Before I could say anything else, he stopped and pivoted to face our attackers. "Please!" he begged me as I took a step past him and tried to skid to a stop. The four wolves were closing in on us, so close I could smell them.

He was right. I hated it, but he was right; I was no use in a fight against wolves when I couldn't shift, and the most helpful thing I could do right now was to get backup.

I ran desperately for the car. I felt two of them break off, bounding after me to the left as Kai moved to intercept them. He was wiry and tough, but smaller than any of the guys who surrounded us. I couldn't waste time running the odds in my mind. I needed to get to the relative safety of the car, so I could call Callum.

My hands shook on the key fob, and I pressed the button just as I reached the door. I threw myself into the slick leather seat and pressed the button desperately to lock the doors, so many times that the car honked at me. A big guy hit the side of my car with his body, but I was already starting the engine.

He smacked the window with his hand. "Hang on! Hear me out."

No way in Hell.

I put it in reverse and when he stayed in my way, I gunned it. The bumper knocked him out of the way, and he stumbled back. I caught his confused expression in the rearview mirror—

Yes, dude, I really did just hit you with my car, take a hint—and I peeled out of there as fast as I could.

But I wasn't leaving Kai. I fished my cell phone out of my purse. My vision felt narrow, and I tried to focus on the road as I dialed Josh.

The phone rang twice, long enough for me to debate giving up and calling Nick or Callum. Finally, Josh picked up. "Hey. Miss me already?"

"We're in trouble," I told him. "Other wolves."

"Get back to the house," he said. In the distance, Callum demanded *what's wrong.*

"Kai's trying to hold them up." There was empty parking lot in front of me, so I swung the car around in the space. "I can't leave him."

"We'll be right there. Piper. *Go.*"

Piper's not my name.

That was a weird thing to pop into my mind.

But maybe *Piper* would have listened.

Whoever the hell I was, I gunned the car back toward the fight.

Read on to find out if Piper saves Kai's butt…

ALSO BY MAY DAWSON

The Lost Fae Series

Wandering Queen

Fallen Queen

Rebel Queen

Lost Queen

Their Shifter Princess:

Their Shifter Princess

Their Shifter Princess 2: Pack War

Their Shifter Princess 3: Coven's Revenge

Their Shifter Academy:

Their Shifter Academy: A Prequel Novella

Their Shifter Academy 1: Unwanted

Their Shifter Academy 2: Unclaimed

Their Shifter Academy 3: Undone

Their Shifter Academy 4: Unforgivable

Their Shifter Academy 5: Unwinnable

Their Shifter Academy 6: Unstoppable

The Wild Angels & Hunters Series:

Wild Angels

Fierce Angels

Dirty Angels

Chosen Angels

Academy of the Supernatural

Her Kind of Magic

His Dangerous Ways

Their Dark Imaginings

Ashley Landon, Bad Medium

Dead Girls Club

Printed in Great Britain
by Amazon

42603642R00129